Gunn gazed at Serena's full lips and squeezed her waist gently. He tilted her head back and kissed her hard. Her mouth opened slightly to Gunn's and, almost in response to her own forwardness, she pulled away.

"Get out of here before I scream!" Serena hissed, her eyes sparkling with anger.

Gunn grinned, tipped his hat, and turned toward his horse.

Click—The sound of a hammer locking into the cocked position.

Serena's Mexican friend stepped out of the shadows.

"No, Pablo," Serena directed, "let him go. He didn't hurt me."

Hackles rose on the back of Gunn's neck. The bitch! She had suckered him, held all the aces, played him against a stacked deck. Gunn untwisted the reins and climbed into the saddle.

"See you again, ma'am," Gunn said, saluting her. "You kiss right good."

Serena stood defiantly, but before she could offer a reply, Gunn had his horse churning into a gallop. . . .

The GUNN Series

by Jory Sherman

#12

THE WIDOWMAKER

GUNN

BY JORY SHERMAN

ZEBRA BOOKS
KENSINGTON PUBLISHING CORP.

DEDICATION

For Sunny and Tom

ZEBRA BOOKS

are published by

KENSINGTON PUBLISHING CORP.
475 Park Avenue South
New York, N.Y. 10016

Printed in the United States of America

CHAPTER ONE

The man called Gunn looked at his face in the mirror.

"Clean as a whistle," said the barber. "I ought to get that hair down another few inches."

"Hair's fine," Gunn winced at his image in the mirror. Not at the image, but at the pain in his jaw. One of the middle teeth. Hurting like a hornet's sting. He didn't give a damn about his hair. It was long, but he liked it that way. Kept his neck warm.

"Planning to stay in El Paso long?"

"Just long enough to get sick of it. You got a tooth-puller in this town? Close by?"

"A dentist, you mean?"

Gunn handed the mirror back to the slim man in the striped shirt, striped suspenders. The shop smelled of talcum powder, bay rum, toilet water and dusty hair. Some of the hair was his own. The barber had taken two inches off and the back of his neck itched. Now, the man produced a duster and began flicking at Gunn's shoulder, tickling his neck with the turkey feathers.

"Yeah."

"Come back after five o'clock and I'll pull it for you." There were six men waiting to get into the chair. All of them glared at Gunn.

"A man could die before five o'clock," Gunn said, easing out of the chair so that he wouldn't hang up his pistol. The chair had been made in Chicago. It was the best half hour he'd spent since riding out of Socorro half a week ago. He dug in his pocket for some bills, but the barber was ignoring him. Looking out the window at a disturbance in the street.

The sounds of the argument drifted through the plate glass window with the legend, Nick's Barber Shop, emblazoned across the pane.

Gunn peeled off a dollar bill, set it on the counter next to the shaving mug and the straight razor. He picked up the bundle of clothes and tried to edge by Nick. Some of the other men waiting got up to look, blocking his way.

It felt good to get out of the buckskins, into some new denims and a shirt that didn't stand up by itself. The buckskins were in the bundle. For a moment he considered leaving them in the waste bin, but a good washing would take some of the trail smell out of them.

"Looks like those boys are giving that dude what works for the Roberts gal a hard way to go."

Gunn looked over the man's shoulder, saw what they were all peering through the window at—three men hazing another on a buckboard. The man on the buckboard looked scared. He was old, a Mexican, and unarmed from what Gunn could see.

"Let me by," said Gunn quietly, his blue-gray eyes flicking back to the men barring his way. "Your money's on the counter, Nick. Keep the change."

The men parted, let him through.

Gunn stepped out onto the rickety boardwalk and started to turn up the street when the woman caught his eye.

She was running across the street toward the buckboard, fighting her skirts to keep from tumbling headlong.

"Stop that!" she shouted. "Stop that you men! Leave Pablo alone!"

The woman had light hair, blonde as honey, wideset brown eyes, a pear-shaped face, dimpled mouth, even white teeth. Gunn took her in at a glance since she was now the center of attention. There was something regal about her bearing, even if she was running full bore toward the disturbance. Running across a dusty street choked with people, horses and carts, wearing a yellow dress with red and green flowers on it, a green bonnet. She was petite, but fiery as a cat with its fur up.

One of the ruffians grabbed the woman's wrist as she came close to the buckboard.

His companions guffawed coarsely.

"Well, naow, Miss Roberts, you're in an all-fired hurry. We're just pokin' a little fun."

Gunn's jaw went granite-hard as he saw the woman's face drain its color. The grip on her wrist obviously hurt her.

The woman twisted and kicked the man who held her in the shin. He cried out in pain and staggered back, hopping on one foot.

One of the other two men reached up and grabbed Pablo by the shirt front, jerked him off the seat of the buckboard. The Mexican's boot struck the brake, hung up there for a second. His assailant pulled on Pablo's arms and he tumbled headfirst into the dirt.

Miss Roberts yelled again.

"You—you bully!"

7

"Keep her out of this, Jack," said the man who had pulled Pablo from the wagon. The man named Jack, who had been shin-kicked, grabbed the woman around the waist, pulled her out of the action. The action was the second man, a burly, thick-necked, bushy-eyebrowed cowhand kicking Pablo in the ribs.

Gunn had seen enough.

Dropping his bundle, he waded into the fray, his six-foot-one frame wedging past a knot of gapers just off the boardwalk. Silently, he grabbed the third man, spun him around. He looked, briefly, into the eyes of a startled young man of medium height with hard blue eyes, freckles over his nose and cheeks. Gunn brought his right fist straight back, drove it straight for the youth's nose. There was a sickening crunch and a squishy sound as if a tomato had been crushed under a boot heel.

Blood spurted from the young man's nose and his eyes frosted over, rolled in their sockets.

His knees gave way and he dropped like a sashweight to the ground. Gunn brought up his knee and cracked him on the point of his jaw. With a sigh, the youth caved in and fell sideways, out of service.

"Look out, Paddy!" shouted Jack, backing away with Miss Roberts. "We got a sidewinder mixin' in!"

Paddy Ryan turned to see the tall, broad-shouldered man in the new duds bearing down on him. Paddy was a red-bearded, square-faced man with a florid face, scraggy orange hair, pug nose. He was solidly built, with a torso hard as a nail keg. He brought up his left arm, cocked his right fist.

Gunn bent over, came in low. He thudded quick fists into Paddy's mid-section, ducked a roundhouse right that whistled over his head. Off-balance, Paddy skidded sideways. Gunn stood up straight, arced a right hand

8

down. His fist cracked into Paddy's jaw, sending his hat flying, shaking sweat out of his glowing orange hair.

Jack Devlin saw his partner execute a flying jig before he bit the dust. He shoved Miss Roberts to one side, lowered his head and charged Gunn. With a grunt, he caught Gunn belt-buckle high, drove him back into the murmuring crowd of spectators.

Gunn went down, Jack atop him.

Fingers clawed at his face. His eyes.

Fingernails pulled skin away from his eyes as the clutch missed. Gunn rolled away and Jack ring-necked him with a powerful arm. Gunn could feel hot breath on the back of his neck. He scrambled, struggling to get on his feet with a hundred and seventy pound man on his back. The arm tightened on his windpipe. Air whistled through Gunn's nose, squeaked in his throat.

With a mighty lunge, Gunn stood up, rammed an elbow straight back. Hard.

The crowd started cheering.

"Get him, Jack!" someone said.

"My money's on the stranger!" yelled another.

Jack wheezed as Gunn's elbow rammed into his ribs, jarred his wind loose from his lungs. He loosened his hold around Gunn's neck and Gunn slipped free.

But Devlin was ready. He socked a short left into Gunn's mouth, staggered him.

Gunn fought for air, shook his head to clear it.

His antagonist swam before his eyes.

Paddy Ryan got his feet under him, swayed groggily in a half-crouch, his blue-green eyes blazing with hatred.

Gunn backed away from Jack, struggling to regain a lost advantage.

Jack powered into him, head lowered, fists flailing. Gunn stepped close, hammered a hard left into the

9

Irisher's gut, smashed a right low, into the groin.

Jack's knees jellied and the steam went out of his rush.

"Finish him off!" yelled someone in the crowd.

"Knock the black Irishman's lights out!" said another.

Gunn heard nothing. He knew he had to finish off the burly man or have Paddy come in to help. He was tiring. His arms filled with lead and his legs turned to stone.

The shadow caught the corner of his eye.

Paddy was up and slinking toward Gunn furtively, deceptively fast on his feet.

Jack had a clear view of Paddy. He leered at Gunn, sure that he had the advantage.

Gunn surprised both men.

He backed away from Jack, ignored him as he turned toward Paddy.

Miss Roberts called out a warning as she helped Pablo to his feet, the forgotten man in the conflict that had now erupted into a full-scale Donnybrook between a stranger and two of the taunters.

"Behind you! Look out!"

Gunn knew Jack was coming fast behind him. He took a full stride, struck out at Paddy who was hunched over, set for the kill.

The blow caught Paddy in the forehead.

The Irishman dropped like a pole-axed steer.

Gunn kept up his momentum, heard the *whish* of a fist past his ear. Jack was right behind him.

"Damn you!" Jack cursed. "Hold still, you bastard."

Gunn sidestepped, dropped to one knee.

The crowd gasped, thinking he was giving up. Jack walked right into it.

Gunn brought his fist up from the ground. Straight.

The fist went in through Jack's arms, connected on the base of his chin. It was a vicious uppercut, snapping

Jack's head back until the spine cracked.

Jack fell in a crumpled heap, air whistling through his nose, eyelids fluttering.

Across the street, in front of the grocery store where Miss Roberts had been a few moments before, a well-dressed Mexican puffed on a thin cigar. His eyes were narrowed to puffed slits, his lower lip pooched out in thought. He wore the clothes of a *caballero*, russet brown trousers, vest and coat, a tasseled sombrero, polished boots, large Spanish-roweled spurs, a gunbelt and pistol. He watched the fight closely, ignoring the gloved Mexican next to him whose face bore no expression at all.

Gunn thought it was over.

Until pain shot through the calf of his leg.

He turned and felt strong hands grab his boot, give his leg a hard twist.

Paddy's bite didn't break the skin, but Gunn fell headlong into the dirt.

A loud roar went up from the crowd, the pros and cons of the shouts mingling as one.

The fall jarred Gun. His hat rolled away lazy.

Paddy twisted again, his hands still gripping Gunn's boot.

Gunn went with the twist, then lashed out. His boot came free, but he missed his target.

Scrambling away, Gunn rose to his feet.

Paddy rushed him on all fours.

The knife blade flashed silver in his hand.

At Paddy's lunge, Gunn leaped up. He came down hard with both boot heels. Dug into Paddy's back, into the kidneys.

Paddy screamed.

The knife slithered out of his hand.

Gunn jumped off, stepped back.

"You learn hard, Mick," he said, aiming a kick.

He caught Paddy in the temple. Paddy slobbered as his eyes glazed. Then he slumped into unconsciousness.

It was all over. Finally.

None of the three men moved.

The gloved Mexican looked at the *caballero*.

"Don Diego," he said softly, "do you want me to. . . ."

"No, Rubio, not now," said Don Diego Torreon. "But we will keep an eye on that *gringo*. See if you can find out who he is when this is over."

Rubio Amargo nodded, flexed his gloved fingers. He was a powerfully built, short-statured man with bronze-black skin, a full moustache, porcine eyes.

Without another word, Torreon walked up the boardwalk, away from the crowd who pressed into the street, all trying to clap Gunn on the back, shake his hand.

Gunn retrieved his hat, was putting it on, trying to acknowledge a torrent of greetings, trying to stand up under all the back-patting.

A small hand touched his arm.

"I'm Carrie Roberts," said a voice, "and I think I'd better take you away from all this. Do you have a horse?"

Gunn nodded, turned and looked into her frank brown eyes.

"As soon as Pablo loads the wagon, meet us at the corner of Hidalgo and Flores. I want to thank you for defending us."

"No need, ma'am, I. . . ."

"Please," she said urgently, "I insist." Her hand tightened on his arm. "You must have supper with us."

Before Gunn could protest, she was gone and the crowd blotted her out of his sight.

Someone handed Gunn his bundle of clothes.

Others pulled the unconscious men out of the street.

Gunn saw a man at the edge of the crowd looking at him intently.

A heavy-set Mexican who wore skin-tight calf-skin gloves on his hands.

The gloved man looked away quickly when Gunn met his glance.

Then disappeared.

Gunn frowned, dusted himself off and forced his way through the lingering crowd to his horse.

A man jostled against him. A familiar face.

Nick, the barber.

"Don't know who you are, mister," he said, "but you been decent. I figure no one else will tell you, so it's up to me. If you can take a little friendly advice, that is."

Gunn stopped walking.

"I'll listen," he said.

"Those boys hazing that Mex. Know who they was?"

Gunn shook his head.

. "Some of Torreon's boys. I'd keep an eye out. Two eyes."

Nick was gone before Gunn could question him further. Someone asked to buy him a drink, but he put the man off. The wagon was rumbling down the street, Pablo and Carrie Roberts sitting on the seat, the back loaded with cartons and sacks of groceries. He had a block to walk to the place where his horse, Duke, was hitched. And then he had to find Hidalgo and Flores, wherever that was.

Behind him, the gloved man, Rubio Amargo, followed, staying to the shadows.

But Gunn wasn't paying attention.

His tooth had started to throb again.

CHAPTER TWO

Carrie Roberts was waiting in the buckboard.

Flores and Hidalgo was on the west end of town. The false fronts and adobes had petered out and the road forked there, the main part stretching toward open country.

"I'm glad you decided to come," said Carrie, smiling. "I hope you don't have other plans."

"Well, I. . . ."

"Good. El Paso will be talking about you all night, and I want to steal you away for myself. Again, Pablo and I thank you. You probably saved his life."

"Who were those men?"

"We can talk about that at the hacienda. There's someone very special I want you to meet."

"Who?"

"A lady. Serena Paxton. She'll be our guest of honor, but I've decided that you must share that honor. I'm sorry. I don't even know your name."

"Gunn."

"Is that all? Just Gunn?"

"Just Gunn."

****

The Mexican watched the buckboard move down the road, followed by the big man on the dun horse.

There was no need to follow. He knew where they were going.

To the hacienda of Carrie Roberts.

El Guante stepped out of the shadows of the overhanging roof. It had not been hard to follow the *gringo*, but it was a long walk back to the hotel where Don Diego Torreon waited for his report.

Rubio Amargo did not hurry as he walked back up the street. There was never any hurry. He was a patient man who liked to have time alone, to flex his gloved fingers. He always wore gloves. That is why they called him *El Guante*—the glove. He was proud of the nickname. It showed that people respected him, feared him. He liked that.

Rubio was a short man and he didn't like that. He had endured the taunts of children and the whispered insults of men when he finally became old enough to wear long trousers. And, when he became old enough to make his own way in the world, he became old enough to kill.

That was what Rubio did best. Kill.

He had developed his muscles on the cattle ranches of Mexico, and on the long drives from Texas to Kansas. He was always careful of his hands, always wore gloves. He didn't like to hit with his fists. Rather, he learned that size and stature meant nothing. If a man was strong and quiet, he could overcome his enemies. All such a man had to do was be patient. Wait for darkness. In the dark, men were all the same size; all children. The advantage came with boldness and cunning.

El Guante was a man who used the night to advantage. And the gloved hands that could span a man's throat,

15

tighten down on the windpipe like a bulldog's relentless bite.

That was what Rubio did best, at night.

No one had ever caught him. But, secretly, the men who had known him over the years knew why he wore gloves. Why he was slow to anger, almost never mixed it up in a fight. But the men who had insulted him had all died in their sleep. Or at least during the night.

So it was that a kind of fear built up around Rubio and his ever-gloved hands. A mystique.

And his own legend made him all the stronger. For now, men did not insult him nor taunt him. Not to his face. Not within hearing. Not men who knew *El Guante*, what he could do with those powerful hands and corded arms.

Rubio stopped in at a store to look at gloves. None were what he wanted. He owned many pairs, but the best were made of soft doeskin sewed delicately together without thick seams underneath. Plain gloves dyed black were his favorite. Lately he had begun buying the leather from Indians, having them sewed to exact fit by a glove-maker in El Paso. Still, he always looked at ready-made gloves, tried them on if they struck his fancy. Today, none did.

This was not the part of town that Rubio liked. There were too many people, too much hurry. It was too bright on the street and the sun hurt his eyes. The thoroughfare was crowded with wagons, horses, people crossing back and forth. The *gringo* smell was strong in his nostrils. He much preferred his own side of town, sitting in *El Maguey*, drinking *tepache*, looking at the pretty women, telling the jokes. Laughing. Even that place was getting to be no good. With the Irishmen that Don Diego had hired coming in there, pawing over the women, getting drunk.

16

Well, the Irishmen had not done well this day. One man had bested three of them. In public.

The thought made Rubio smile.

As he passed a man on the boardwalk, he saw the man staring at him.

Rubio pulled his hatbrim lower and scowled.

Fucking *gringos!*

****

Don Diego Torreon did not live in El Paso, but across the border, in Ciudad Juarez. Yet, he had interests on the American side. Many interests.

Now, in the hotel room he rented whenever he had business in El Paso, he waited impatiently for Rubio Amargo.

The Hotel Flores was pretentious. Close enough to the border to stand out when Mexicans came across, it seemed to stand haughtily aloof from the surrounding buildings, those less favored on the Mexican side. But Don Diego liked it because they did not ask many questions and they gave him better service than he would get uptown, even with his money.

Now, the room resembled a pig sty.

Jack Devlin was looking sheepishly out the second floor window, holding one hand up to his head. Wondering what had happened to him.

Paddy Ryan was pouring his third drink from the bottle of whiskey Don Diego had had sent up from the saloon downstairs. Alfie Sloan's nose was still bleeding. The floor was littered with bloody towels, the room reeked of cigar smoke and sweat.

"I'll kill that sumbitch," muttered Alfie, who was not

17

as young as he looked. He still had the freckles of childhood, but that only made him more dangerous. He was twenty-one, and deadly. Or he wouldn't be there.

Don Diego looked at them, his face an expressionless mask. Alfie leaned back in his chair, trying to stop the bleeding. His nose was swollen and his eyes red-rimmed.

"You won't kill shit," said Paddy. "Did you even see the waddie what laid into yer?"

"Paddy, godamnit, I just turned around and everything went black." Alfie had a high-pitched squeaky voice that, like the freckles, had lingered after adolescence. To laugh at him was dangerous. The youth had a hair-trigger temper. The only man he feared was Paddy. Maybe *El Guante*, a little. He didn't like Mexicans, but Don Diego paid well, and he promised a lot more.

Jack Devlin turned away from the window.

"Rubio's comin'," he said laconically.

Don Diego didn't move from the large wing-backed chair. He sat there, with his legs crossed, drawing thoughtfully on his cigar. He tapped the ashes off in a cuspidor near one of the legs.

"Maybe we'll find out who that cocksucker was," said Alfie, leaning forward to see if his nose had stopped bleeding.

"Maybe," said Jack, pacing the floor nervously. He didn't like it. They were supposed to rag old Pablo and put some fear into the Roberts woman. What had started out in fun had ended in humiliation.

"You ever see that bugger before, Don Diego?" asked Paddy, his words starting to slur. There was a lilting reminder of the "auld sod" in his voice, but the re in his speech was also the flat drawl of a westerner.

Don Diego sighed, looked at Paddy. He felt embarrassed for him and for the others. It was not manly to lose like that. He had expected much more of them. Still, the man who had come out of the barber shop was no ordinary man. He had struck from nowhere. Fast, hard. It was true that he was a foot taller than Paddy, a head taller than Jack Devlin, and he outweighed the young-looking one, Alfie, by thirty pounds at least. But three men had gone down and it was just as well no one knew they worked for him.

"No," said Torreon slowly, "I do not know this man, but I have seen his kind before. He is a drifter, a stranger. He wore the new clothes so that you could not see the trail dust on the cloth. But there is grit in the pores of his skin and you can see that he has been on a long trail and that he looks over his shoulder like a man hunted."

"No owlhoot's gonna mix in where he don't belong," argued Paddy.

"Damn right!" underlined the kid, Alfie. They still called him a kid, although they knew well that he was full growed.

"He didn't have no color in his eyes," said Jack, shaking his head. Sometimes Jack drifted off and said things no one could understand.

"Huh?" asked Paddy, scraping the bottle across the table as he brought it to his glass for another pour.

"Nothin'," said Jack, looking past Torreon in a thirty-yard stare. "He had eyes like blue glass. Like icicles."

"Jesus," said Alfie.

"Hell, he was probably crazy," said Paddy, trying to convince himself. "No man on the run mixes in like that I tell you. Crazy."

"No," said Don Diego. "Whoever that man was, he was not crazy. The three of you are very lucky this day that you are still alive. He is a man who could kill very easily I think. Jack is right. He had the pale eyes and I think if one of you had drawn a pistol you would not be here in this room."

A silence settled over the Irishers. Don Diego blew a spool of blue smoke through his pudgy lips, shifted his weight in the chair.

There was a knock on the door.

Alfie opened it.

Rubio stepped in, looked at the Irishmen as if they were bugs. They looked back at him, trying to erase the sheepishness from their faces.

"Close the door," said Don Diego to Alfie.

The door slid shut as if Alfie was afraid to break the silence that drifted in and out like breath.

"Well?" asked Don Diego, looking up at the round-faced Rubio. "What did you learn today, my friend?"

Rubio stood there, anchored solidly, flexing his gloved fingers.

"The *gringo* went to the Roberts hacienda with the woman and Pablo."

"Why?"

Rubio shrugged.

"I do not know."

"Did he know the woman before?"

"I do not think so, *patron*."

"What is the man's name? Did you find that out?"

"No, *patron*. No one knows this man. He rides a dun horse that is many hands high. He carries a Winchester on his saddle and he wears a knife. I think he knows how to use the Colt in his holster."

"Do you think he has come because of Paxton?"

Rubio shrugged.

This time he had nothing to say.

The silence slid back in like a sheet being pulled over an empty bed.

Paddy coughed, choking on the whiskey.

Jack stared into space, at a spot yards beyond Rubio's head.

Alfie looked around at everyone, wondering.

"Well, Jesus," said the kid. "What if he is here over that? He's no better'n us. I didn't even see him coming for Chrissakes."

"Shut up, Alfie," said Paddy. "Button your dumb kid lip."

Alfie's freckled face reddened, but he backed off, kept his peace.

"Purty ladies," said Jack, to no one.

"What is it you are saying?" asked Don Diego, suddenly interested. He leaned forward in his chair.

"Man likes the gals." Jack looked at Torreon, their eyes meeting in a kind of understanding. "He just went off with Carrie Roberts to dip his wick."

Torreon smiled.

Slapped his knee soundly with the flat of his left palm.

"Ah, Jack, I think you are right. He saw the woman in peril and, like a *caballero*, he did the battle for her. That is it, no? You, Rubio, what do you think of this grand idea?"

Rubio looked uncomfortable. He shifted the weight on his feet.

"I do not think he knows the woman and probably he has not heard of the Paxton matter. But the woman will tell him and when we stoop to pick the vegetables there will be a snake in the garden."

Torreon sighed again.

And the silence settled back in the room, hung in the stale air, with the reek of whiskey and smoke, like

21

something heavy and imponderable.

****

The hacienda was a sprawling adobe on a long sloping hillside with a commanding view of the valley. Logs jutted out of the flat planes of the massive house. The barred windows were framed with climbing vines. Cactus and flowers bloomed everywhere Gunn looked. Horses and cattle grazed in the pastures, and men waved at the wagon as it rumbled up the road, streaming twin spools of dust from its wheels.

Carrie climbed down from the seat after the wagon stopped. Pablo clucked to the horse, followed the road around the side of the house.

"What do you think of it?" asked Carrie.

"Mighty nice," said Gunn, already feeling out of place. He could smell the blooming flowers, see the courtyard beyond the arched gate.

"Come inside. I'll fix us a cool drink."

Gunn took off his leather hat, slapped it against his thigh. The new clothes were still stiff, but comfortable. His tooth pain had ebbed to a dull throb. He tried not to worry it with his tongue. It was loose and likely wouldn't hold up much longer. He felt the aches from the fight more than the tooth now. The ride from town had loosened him up some, but now he felt the places where the blows had landed. His leg bothered him where Paddy had bit him.

He followed Carrie through the gate, over the flagstone path in the courtyard to the patio. They entered the house, went through an indoor patio before coming to the spacious living room. It was cool inside, bright with color. There were flowers in huge clay vases and Indian blankets adorning the bare walls. There were Conquistador artifacts and Mexican paintings on some of the walls. The furniture was wood and leather. It smelled nice in the room.

"Have a chair and I'll have the *criada* bring us some *tepache*. Do you know the drink?"

"Yes. Where do you get the pineapple from?"

"Oh, we make it with bananas too. Those come from New Orleans, the pineapples from La Ciudad de los Angeles."

She laughed and left Gunn alone. He sat in a square-backed chair, stretched out his feet. The shine on his boots was long gone, the toes scuffed. It didn't matter. He wouldn't be there long. He still had his room at the Flores Hotel and he wanted to provision for the next leg of his aimless journey. California, maybe, with no particular destination in mind. San Diego, maybe, where he could smell the sea and swim in the ocean.

Gunn's thoughts were wiped away when she came into the room.

The woman startled him.

He had been expecting Carrie, but this was not Carrie.

"Hello," she said. "Who are you?"

Gunn swallowed, struggled for his voice.

It wouldn't come.

She laughed, started toward him, stretching out a delicate hand.

"I'm Serena Paxton," she said. "Don't worry. I won't bite you."

But she had bitten him.

Hard.

CHAPTER THREE

Serena Paxton waited for Gunn to take her hand.

He rose from his chair, stood there, awe-struck. His pale blue eyes clouded with fleeting shadows. His lips quivered.

Serena was beautiful. Tall, almost as tall as he. She had blue-green eyes, long dark hair with tresses that fell past her shoulders, almost to the curve of her high rounded buttocks. She was dressed in riding breeches, boots, a blouse that strained to bursting from partially visible breasts that pushed against the cloth. Her eyes danced with light. Dainty dimples framed her mouth. Her nose was thin, patrician, the nostrils as finely chiseled as carvings.

Finally, she thrust her hand in Gunn's. He held it limply as if afraid it would shatter.

"Cat got your tongue?" she teased.

Gunn tried to swallow the lump that jammed his throat, strangled him.

Not since Laurie had he seen a woman who affected him so much.

Laurie.

His wife. Dead these three long years. Gone forever

and her memory still strong at times. Like now, with someone named Serena standing so close he could smell the lavendar flower in her dark hair, the musk that seemed to emanate from her lean willowy presence. A feminine scent, heady and overpowering. Like desert nights or summer meadows in the mountains.

Serena's face wrinkled in puzzlement.

Carrie Roberts entered the room, carrying three glasses on a wooden tray. The glasses shimmered with amber light, and the scent of pineapple permeated the room.

"Oh, I see you two have met," she said.

"Not exactly," said Serena. "I saw this man sitting here and introduced myself. So far he hasn't said a single word."

Carrie stopped, looked at Gunn's face. A look of fleeting sadness crossed her own, was quickly replaced by a smile.

"Serena, this is Gunn. He's going to be our guest for supper tonight. He saved Pablo from a severe beating in town a while ago. I know he speaks. I've heard him talk."

Gunn winced at Carrie's chiding.

"Yes, Gunn," he blurted. "I—I'm glad to meet you, ma'am."

"Well, now," laughed Serena. "You can speak. What's the matter? Did I shock you that much?"

Gunn bowed his head, flushed with shame.

"I—I don't rightly know what came over me, ma'am. You walked in here and I wasn't expecting you. I'm sorry."

Serena touched him on the arm.

"Don't be sorry. I like strong silent men. So, tell me, what happened in town?"

"First, we'll sit down and sip our drinks," said Carrie matter-of-factly. "The *tepache* is cool now, right out of the *olla*."

Gunn and Serena accepted the proffered drinks. Gunn sat after the women had seated themselves on the divan. He squirmed while Carrie told Serena of the fight and his part in it. But Carrie was brief and she didn't embellish the facts much.

"That was manly of you to defend Carrie," said Serena, eyeing Gunn with renewed interest. He found it very disconcerting to look at her. He wondered if she was aware of her own beauty. Probably not. It was a natural beauty and he noticed that she did not use rouge on her lips or cheeks. She seemed, he thought, very self-assured, but there was also an air of troubled worry in her eyes that he had noticed while Carrie was telling her about the three men who had picked on Pablo.

"Seemed to me the Mexican was outnumbered," said Gunn. "And the one jasper was mighty rough on Miss Roberts."

"I was afraid something like that would happen," said Serena. "Do you suppose they know I'm back, that I'm staying with you, Carrie?"

"It could be," said Carrie. "Torreon has eyes everywhere in El Paso."

Torreon.

Gunn had heard the name before. Where? When?

Then, he remembered.

Nick, the barber.

He looked at Carrie, barely concealing his curiosity. "Who is this Torreon?" he asked.

"You've heard of him?" Carrie moved to the edge of

the divan as if about to leap at him. "Don Diego Torreon?"

"Barber in town. Told me those were Torreon's men. Never heard of him before."

Serena's eyes narrowed.

"Just where do you come from, Mister Gunn?" she asked, an icy tone creeping into her voice. "I don't believe Carrie mentioned it."

Gunn felt the sudden chill in the room.

"All over," he said. "And nowhere."

"I see."

This time Serena did not conceal her hostility. Instead, she rose from the divan without finishing her drink and slammed the glass down on the low table next to the tray.

"Please excuse me, Carrie. I'd like to freshen up. It's been a long morning and I'm weary from the trip."

Before Carrie could say anything, Serena was gone. Carrie stared after her, a puzzled look on her face.

For a long moment, neither of them said anything.

Gunn didn't know what to say.

He was stunned at Serena's abrupt departure. He knew it had something to do with him, but he could not fathom a reason. Had he offended her in some way? Did she disbelieve him? It was possible. The name Torreon came to mind. He had heard it mentioned twice today. Once in town, and now here, at the hacienda. Yet he had never heard the name before. Serena must know him or have had dealings with him to have reacted the way she had. It was puzzling. All of it.

"Maybe I'd better leave," he said to Carrie. He had not finished the *tepache*. The taste lingered in his mouth. The beverage was mildly alcoholic and he did not feel any of its effects. It was a cool drink, seemed perfectly suited to such a fine house, such a fine room.

"No, Gunn, please. Don't go." There was pleading in Carrie's voice. "Serena didn't mean anything. She's upset. The mere mentio of Torreon's name is enough to set her off. You can't blame her. Really, you can't."

"I don't believe I mentioned him." Gunn was immediately sorry at the sarcasm that had crept into his voice. He felt snubbed by Serena. The woman had rocked him off his bootheels and then rejected him. Or had seemed to. That sometimes happened. When a man wanted to make an impression on a particular person he often ruined things by acting the fool involuntarily. That's the way he felt now. As if he'd been a fool.

"No, of course not. I didn't mean that." Carrie's voice dropped to a conspiratorial level. She leaned toward Gunn. "Serena has been through a lot. Perhaps I should have explained before you met her. I—I guess it's my fault. I didn't realize that Torreon's men would go this far to torment her friends."

"You'll have to explain that."

"Serena has been in eastern Texas on a cattle buying trip. She arrived back early this morning. From San Antonio. She didn't show you her grief, but the news that brought her back was sad. Her father, Anthony Paxton, was murdered two weeks ago. Both Serena and her mother, Winifred, will leave for their ranch in the morning."

"Serena's mother is here?"

"Yes. Too distraught to see anyone right now. But, she'll be at supper. She's a strong woman."

"Odd to send a woman on a cattle buying trip, isn't it?"
Carrie laughed.

"You don't know Serena! She can ride and shoot better than a lot of men. She knows cattle. The Paxtons survived in this country, as did we all, by being tenacious, strong, versatile."

"Until now."

"Yes, until now. Gunn, I don't like it. You're probably not interested in our troubles. I just wanted you to know that Serena and Winifred are returning under the worst of circumstances. Anthony is gone and they'll be alone—struggling to hold on to their lands against severe odds."

"Torreon?"

Carrie nodded.

Gunn was in no hurry to leave now. Carrie's account of Anthony Paxton's murder had him hooked. The man had left a widow and orphan and they appeared to be an unusual pair of women.

"Anthony Paxton was not the first man to leave a widow on Luna Creek," said Carrie. "There have been others."

She bowed her head, stared into her glass of *tepache*.

"You?" he asked quietly.

Carrie nodded.

"Yes. I'm a widow. Didn't you know? No, of course not. My husband, Eugene, was slain a year ago. He was the first."

"The first? Was Paxton the second?"

A wry smile flickered on Carrie's lips.

"No. Only the latest. There were several families, including my husband and I, who settled on these lands some ten years ago. Along Luna Creek. The titles were clear, so we thought. Part of a Spanish Land Grant. At first, we homesteaded, then Eugene, who had some training in the law, cleared the titles, saw to it that all of the families had deeds. The land is fertile, good grazing for livestock, plenty of water. The homesteaders even built a town. Palomas. About a year and a half ago, Torreon said that the lands were his and produced a document to back up his claim. Eugene claimed that it was a forgery. He went to Austin, doublechecked, and saw that Torreon's claim to the lands was based on some confusion of ownership dating back some years. But, we lived on the land, made it what it is today."

"Did the courts decide on the present ownership?"

"No. It never came to that. Mainly because the lands in question are not in Texas, but in New Mexico. Or Mexico. Until a surveying team comes in to decide it, that's where we stand. Eugene was on his way to Sante Fe the night he was killed to try and straighten things out."

"So how does Torreon justify his claim?"

"He has a document, even if it's either a forgery or invalid. But he has resorted to violence and intimidation in order to move onto our lands."

"How? Do you have proof?"

Carrie looked at him sadly.

"We can't prove a thing. Shortly after Eugene was killed, the nightriders started in. We don't know who they are. Crops were burned, cattle slaughtered. Warnings posted on fences. Palomas has become a fear-filled town. The killings are all planned. We know that. By the widowmakers."

"Widowmakers?"

"Yes. Only the heads of households are murdered. There are a lot of widows along Luna Creek, Gunn. I'm one of them. Winifred is another. Now."

Gunn looked at Carrie, a wave of sympathy stirring his senses. He was beginning to form a picture in his mind.

Torreon wanted the land where the homesteaders had lived for a decade. Land that had been improved by them and was now worth much more than when it lay fallow and undeveloped. Even Roberts had been confused, apparently, about titles. From what he had discerned, Luna Creek lay in New Mexico, not Texas. Yet the original land grant deeds must have been part of Texas. Such matters were not easily unraveled. But for a man to take the law into his own hands, murder the homesteaders, was not only an injustice, but vile and cowardly. Possession was still nine-tenths of the law in the West.

"Why did those men attack Pablo this morning?" Gunn asked. "That doesn't seem to fit the pattern."

"I know. It didn't make sense. Except that others along Luna Creek have reported trouble in El Paso. And, some have lost good hands because of being beaten up by those Irishmen who apparently work for Torreon. I guess Torreon wants to run all the men off so he can move in. He thinks it will be easy to take the land away from women."

"Will it?"

"No!" Carrie half-rose from her seat. "We'll fight him! We're not afraid!"

"Good," said Gunn, amazed at her spunk. "But you can't do it alone."

"Will you help us?" she asked eagerly.

"I might. But I'll have to find out a lot more than I know now before I take on Torreon."

Carrie's face lit up. She finished her *tepache*, rose from the divan. She went to Gunn, pecked him on the cheek. The light kiss was fleeting, but he tingled as she danced away, her skirts rustling as she did a small pirouette.

"Serena and Winifred will be thrilled. But you must be careful. I was hoping you'd help us in our plight. Luna Creek and Palomas needs a man like you, Gunn. One who is not afraid of Torreon and his ruffians."

Gunn stood up, said nothing for a few moments. He didn't want to spoil Carrie's enthusiasm. But there were a lot of unanswered questions. He had to find out more about Torreon, the Irishers who were working for him.

"I'm not saying I will help, Carrie," he said, finally. "But I will look around and see what I can find out. I was considering an offer to drive a herd of cattle up the Goodnight-Loving for a friend of mine, Jed Randall."

"Jed Randall? I know him. But how long has it been since you've heard from him?"

"Two months. Three."

Carrie stood stockstill in the center of the room, her gaiety gone.

"Why? Somethin' wrong?"

"Gunn, that herd Jed was going to take up the Goodnight-Loving was ours—the whole valley's. And there isn't going to be any cattle drive this fall. There weren't enough hands to do the roundup right and too many cattle had been rustled this year. We missed the Spring drive entirely. That's why Jed got in touch with you. We hoped to make a Fall drive, beat the winter, but it's too late now."

She was right, Gunn knew. This was November. Winter had come to some parts of the country already. The Goodnight-Loving went up the Pecos to Pueblo and Denver. It would be pure hell crossing the Pecos after a rain, then the Canadian, hoping the passes would be clear instead of choked with six foot drifts.

"You might get up the Western, to Dodge," Gunn

said. "Pick up the Atchison, Topeka out of Pueblo there. Have to hurry like hell."

"No, it's not worth the risk," said Carrie. "Some of the ranchers would lose everything. Best to try for a Spring roundup and a heavy drive then. It's the only chance we have. So you see, we need you here, Gunn. I'll match whatever Jed was going to pay you."

"I'll double it," said a voice.

Gunn's head twisted in the direction of the voice.

His jaw dropped.

Heart pumped faster.

She stood in the arched doorway like a queen. Her long flowing dress was black as coal, trimmed in shiny lace. Her black hair was streaked down the center with a wide band of silver gray. She had the look of a hawk in her eyes. The thin nose seemed to be chiseled out of granite. The mouth was firm, full-lipped, the chin small and delicately rounded. She carried a sheaf of roses in her hands.

"You'll stay, Mister Gunn," she said softly, but her voice carried across the room with ease. "I'm Mrs. Anthony Paxton and I know a man when I see one."

For the second time that day, Gunn was dumbstruck, speechless.

CHAPTER FOUR

Mort Wallen crossed the ford at Luna Creek. He was bone-tired and angry. But the cattle were gathered on the lower pasture and the men almost finished. If they would stick it out. It was a new moon night and none of them liked it much, being out there with a full herd in the darkness. Not after what had happened that day.

He couldn't brood about it, though. The cattle were close. He would hear if anything went wrong.

He worked the sorrel up the wide path, saw the top of his adobe over the rise. The setting sun had turned the clay pink. His wife stood outside, waving to him. Behind her, the children waved too. They had been watching, he knew, as the long line of cattle had come bawling out of the hills, fanned out over the grass on the other side of the creek.

The scent of wood smoke filled the air and he saw a thin curl of smoke spiraling out of the chimney. He was proud of the land, his family, the modest dwelling they had built from rammed earth ten years before. His eyes swept to the corrals, the outbuildings. Horses nickered. Not the Arabian stock like the Paxtons had, but good bottomed horses that did the work.

He waved back, but his wave was not cheerful.

His arm weighed a ton and his shoulders ached something fierce.

And the news was bad.

"What's wrong, Mort?" Sally asked as he rode up.

"Nothing," he said. "Everything's fine."

But a shadow crossed her face and she bit her lip. She looked up at her husband with concern. Mort's thick eyebrows were flocked with dust and there were smudges under his red-rimmed eyes. His square shoulders sagged and his cracked lips drooped in a frown. Sweat circles stained his shirt around the armpits.

Sally was a petite woman with a pinched face whose hair had begun turning gray the past year. She wiped a strand of it away as she gathered the boy and girl next to her. Little Malcolm was four years old and smiled tentatively up at his daddy. Jennifer was six and she looked more like her father, with steady brown eyes, sandy hair and the blunt nose. Malcolm had the small bones of his mother, the smallish face that seemed like a living cameo framed by long brown hair.

Mort swung down, kissed Jennifer first, then hugged Malcolm.

Sally waited for him to hold her and kiss her, but he walked on by her, leading the sorrel.

"You children go inside, set the table. I'll be in directly. I want to talk to your father first."

"Yes'm," said Jennifer. Malcolm pouted until jerked by his sister who dragged him into the house.

Mort loosened the cinches, slipped the saddle from the sorrel's back, turned him into a corral. Then he took off the bridle. The horse trotted to the hay trough, shaking the sweat off his body.

"I'll rub him down directly," Mort said to Sally, who had come up beside him. He leaned down, picked up the saddle, lugged it to the tack room a few yards away.

"Usually you rub him down before you turn him in," she said. Not nagging. Gently reminding him that she was there. That she knew something was wrong.

"Usually."

"Mort, what's wrong?"

"I told you. . . ."

He slammed the saddle down hard on a wood horse, slapped the bridle onto a nail with a rattle of leather.

"Morton Wallen, don't lie to me. Now I don't want the children upset, so you'd better get it off your chest now. Or you'll go in there and be grouchy all during supper."

Mort sighed, looked at his wife. He took her in his arms, held her against him for a long moment.

"No kiss?" she pouted.

He smiled wanly, leaned down and kissed her.

"The three Mexes quit today," he blurted. "Claudio said he'd draw his pay in the morning. I wrote 'em out vouchers on the spot."

Sally was taken aback.

"Claudio? What about Fernando?"

"Yeah, Fernando too. And that Portillo, new hired a month back."

"But we practically raised Fernando."

"Well, somethin's up. Claudio wouldn't tell me. He just acted scared and I think he scared hell out of Fernando and Portillo. Anyways, they up and left after the gather. Didn't want to help with the drive."

"I didn't see them come back to the bunkhouse."

"No. I reckon they moved their stuff out last night or early this mornin'. Just picked up their bundles after I let

36

'em go. Sneaky."

Sally put her arm on his, led him out of the tack room. Mort didn't bother to close the door.

A pair of doves whistled by as the sun sank over the horizon. Their wings whistled like tiny flutes piping. The creek swarmed with ribbony colors, streaks of gold and orange, red and gray. Cattle bawled and the voices of men carried on the still air as they settled the herd down, spreading them out along the creek's deeper parts so they wouldn't stray across.

"The Paxtons will be back tomorrow," she said. "You can talk to Winifred and Serena about it then. We can all go into town, make a day of it."

Her cheery attitude helped. Mort gave her arm a squeeze.

He wanted things to be all right. Sally must know, though, that there was some reason behind the Mexicans quitting like that. You couldn't sweep it under the rug, or out the door.

"Same as it was the last time, when Anthony was killed," he said as they walked toward the house. Mort had been adding rooms to the house over the years so that it was bigger than it looked from the outside. It was still only one-storied, but now there was an inner courtyard, a patio where they felt secure when the front door was bolted. Sally had flowers growing there and he had put up eaves so that they could sit outside on rainy days and watch the rain splatter on the flagstone table in the center.

"You don't know that," said Sally quickly. Too quickly.

"Tony Paxton let five men go the day he was killed. The night. And it was a new moon night."

"Tonight's a new moon." There was a quaver in her voice as she stopped outside the front door. Inside, there was the faint tinkle of dishes and eating utensils. The Wallens had no servants.

"I know, Sal."

Inside, while Mort washed up in the kitchen from the bowl and pitcher Sally always had set out for him, the children completed setting the table. Sally moved pots around on the wood stove using heavy potholders she had sewed herself, dyed burlap over cotton batting.

"The table's set, Mommy," announced Jennifer. "Malcolm has to go pee."

"Take him out the back. And hurry."

Mort chuckled. It was easy to forget his troubles once inside the house. Steam rose from the big pot when Sally lifted the lid, stirred the contents with a ladle.

"Umm, smells good," said her husband, setting his hat on the counter while he washed his face. "Beef stew?"

"Yes, Morton. I had to use up the carrots before they went pithy. There's potatoes and biscuits to go with."

"Good. I'm plumb starved."

Sally looked shyly at her husband, noting his nervous manner. He had not gone to the bunkhouse as he usually did and he was still wearing the converted Remington New Model Army .44 pistol. It was his habit to hang the gunbelt up when he entered the house. It was his habit to see that Cookie sent chuck down to the boys minding the herd. Now, his gaze wandered to the window and he seemed reluctant to lay the towel aside and go into supper.

"Was there any other trouble up in the hills?" she asked.

"No trouble," he said quickly.

"But there was something."

"Yes. Sign. A cold camp up there, less'n a day old. Tracks."

"Are you going to wear your pistol to supper?"

Mort's face flushed a deep red under his tan.

"Forgot," he mumbled, as he unbuckled the belt, rebuckled it. He took it to a hook in the living room, next to the door. Sally banked the fire in the firebox, twisted the damper on the stove pipe.

Mort stood before the fireplace in the living room, gazing at the empty hearth.

"Are you going to send Cookie out to the pasture with some chuck for the boys?"

Mort jumped a foot at the sound of Sally's voice.

"Uh, no," he said. "They're comin' in. No use to have 'em out there now."

"You mean because nothing will happen?"

"I mean, dammit," he exploded, "that it wouldn't do any good now."

Sally bit her lip. She didn't want to nag Mort. But she was frightened now. She knew what he was thinking. The attacks always came well after the sun was down. It was still early. Mort, in his concern for his men, didn't want any of them hurt. He would go out there after supper to see if they followed his orders and went back out to the herd. He had left it up to them. They had all seen the sign, too.

"But they'll be out there later?"

"Sally, you're pokin' mighty hard. Charlie's stayin' with the herd during supper. Rafe and Clem will bring him some grub."

"I'm sorry, Mort. Supper's on and I just wanted you to relax so you won't choke on your food. I didn't mean to pry into your business."

Mort softened.

"Come here," he said gruffly. Sally went to him eagerly, fell into his arms. She shuddered with pleasure as he squeezed her.

"I love you," she said.

"I know. I'm sorry, Sal. Jumpy, I guess. I can't force the boys to ride nightherd, but I want 'em to. Might help, if they come." He looked up at the rifle over the mantel, considered whether to take it down, set it by the front door. He had left the other Winchester in its boot in the tackroom. Where it would be handy. But, if they stormed the house. . . .

"Let's eat," said Sally, slipping her arms away from his waist.

Mort decided to leave the rifle where it was. He chastised himself for his indecision, but he was trying to think of his family's feelings too. Sally was mighty sharp and she noticed every little thing. Maybe that's what irritated him now. She didn't miss much and he wanted it to be a normal evening.

But he couldn't deny that things were not right.

He ate supper in stony silence, forcing a smile now and then which did not fool his children nor his wife. Every time a spoon struck a dish or a cup rattled against a saucer, Mort jerked as if shot. He skipped the apple cobbler dessert and went into the living room to light up his pipe. When the children went to bed he hugged them more warmly than usual, seemed reluctant to part with them.

"Mort, do you want some brandy to calm you down?" Sally said much later, after finishing the dishes. "You're some spooked tonight."

"No, Sal. I want to keep my wits about me."

He held the rifle in his hands, levered a shell into the chamber. Working the action seemed to calm him down. He held the rifle up, aimed it at the draped window.

Sally watched him, apprehensive.

"I'll get ready for bed," she said. "You coming?"

"In a while."

Sally started toward the hall doorway, then froze as a shot cracked the still air outside.

Mort's face drained of color.

Sally rushed to him, blocked his way.

"Don't go out there," she pleaded, her voice husky with fear.

"I have to, dammit."

"No!" she screamed.

Mort shoved her aside. He was rougher than he intended to be, and Sally staggered.

Another shot rang out. Far away, as if in a dream. Sally raced after her husband, hiking her skirt up to keep from tripping. Ahead of her, she heard footsteps.

The front door creaked open, banged shut.

"Mort!" she screamed. "Come back!"

But there was only silence.

Sally collapsed on the butcher block in the kitchen, sobbing.

****

Gunn picked at his food.

The three women chatted back and forth as if he wasn't there. The Paxtons in black dresses, Carrie in a subdued gown that only enhanced her natural beauty. A faint tinge of rouge on her cheeks gave her face a liveliness that he hadn't noticed before. Winifred Paxton, her face drenched in a white powder, appeared ghostly in the lamplight. Serena, with her hair swept back away from her face, was dazzlingly beautiful, like something graceful fashioned of fine bone china, her skin almost translucent, her black hair sleek and shining like a fine raiment of exquisite silk.

It was awkward sitting there in his new clothes, listening to them talk about everything under the sun except the murders that were on all their minds. It was as if a truce had been declared. Since meeting Winifred he had felt that he was involved in an elaborate plot to help a pair of widows and an orphan, if Serena at her age could be called that, and if he tried to protest they would lock him in a dungeon and feed him gruel for the rest of his days.

But it wasn't like that at all. The food was plentiful and good. Roast beef, potatoes, biscuits, green beans, hot tortillas, butter, honey, wine, coffee. There was crystal and china and fine silver. He felt out of place, despite the fact that he was out of buckskins and had a haircut.

"I wish you could have known my husband, Mister Gunn," said Winifred abruptly.

"Huh?" Gunn's thoughts had been drifting, and the directly spoken words caught him off guard.

"Anthony Paxton. My husband. He was a pioneer. A rugged man, much like yourself. He was not afraid of anything. Are you afraid of anything, Mister Gunn?"

Gunn blinked, uncertain of where he was now that he'd been drawn into the conversation like a dripping cat pulled from a barrel of rainwater. He looked into Winifred's piercing eyes. His skin crawled. He had the distinct feeling that he was on trial—and Mrs. Paxton was the prosecuting attorney.

"The name's Gunn," he said. "There's no mister in front of it. And, yes, I'm afraid of some things."

"Like what?" Her eyes speared him like a mouse on a shrike's beak.

"Death. Certain women. Disease. Starvation. Getting crippled."

Serena laughed. Her mother fixed her with a stark look of reprimand. Carrie stifled a titter, looked at Gunn with sympathy. For which he was grateful. Winifred sat straight in her chair, crunching up a linen napkin with delicate fingers that seemed exceptionally long and bony.

"Are you afraid to fight for justice?"

"I reckon not," Gunn said drily. "Depends on what justice you're talking about. It's different for everyone. Depends on which side you're on."

"Mister Gunn, or whatever your name is, you must have some sense of morality. Of decency. My husband was killed in the dead of night by a coward. He was killed in darkness by an attacker he never saw. He was strangled like an animal. Carrie's husband was killed the same way. I'm wondering if you're man enough to help. I heard what you did in town today. That was brave. But it was also in broad daylight. I'm prepared to offer you a grant, a gratuity, of two thousand dollars if you will stay on and find my husband's murderer. Carrie Roberts will match that amount. Find him, and kill him!"

Gunn pushed away from the table, glared at Winifred Paxton.

"Mrs. Paxton, I have worked as a range detective, but I was paid a salary like any ordinary man. I'm not a bounty hunter. I have money of my own and I don't need to hunt men to make a decent living."

43

"Then you refuse?"

"I don't like being corralled, Mrs. Paxton, and I feel like I've been herded into a box canyon. I appreciate your offer and I understand your grief, but I think you would do better hiring someone in the line of manhunter."

They all turned as footsteps pounded on the tile floors.

Pablo came rushing in to the dining room, breathless, his face contorted in fear.

"Come quick," he said. "It has happened again. Murder!"

CHAPTER FIVE

Gunn looked at the bloated face of the dead man.

The eyes were bugged out, glistened in the light from the lantern held in Pablo's shaking hand. There were bruises on the neck. The man's face was waxen, the lips blue.

The man was draped over an unsaddled horse, hands and feet tied together. The horse had a hackamore on it. It was a sorrel, lathered from a hard ride. The horse had been led there, Gunn figured, because one of Carrie's hands held onto the hackamore to keep the animal from bolting. The sorrel's eyes flared as it tried to walk out from under the dead man.

Gunn drew his knife, cut the bonds that held the dead man's feet and hands. He lifted the man tenderly from the horse, laid him out flat on the ground. The sorrel sidled away, nickered in fear.

"Get the horse out of here," Gunn said to the Mexican youth. "Anybody know this man?"

He looked up at the balloons of faces bobbing in the amber light from Pablo's lantern.

Winifred Paxton's face was ghost-white, stern. Serena's a mask of forced composure. Carrie Roberts was

45

on the verge of tears.

"It—it's Mort Wallen," she said. "Poor Sally. The children. Oh, Serena, this is awful. Just awful."

Gunn felt the man's neck gingerly. It was broken.

"Hold the lantern close, Pablo," Gunn said. "I want to look at something."

"You ghoul!" said Winifred. "The man's dead. Haven't you any compassion?"

"His neck's broke," said Gunn. "And I want to see if there's any rope burns on his neck."

"Please, go ahead. Do what you have to do." Serena's voice. Stead, lilting. Compassionate.

Pablo held the lantern down close to the dead man's face. His hand shook even more. The veins stood out like earthworms under the surface after a hard rain.

Gunn looked closely at the neck, and then at the front of the man's clothes. Something fluttered in his stomach. Bile rose up in his throat. The man's tongue was wedged in between his teeth. He had gone down fast. Death was quick. Too quick.

He stood up, satisfied. His knees felt rubbery. Death was never pleasant. This death was gruesome. A man should not have to die that way, cut off from life's breath without warning.

"Well, Mister Gunn?" asked Winifred imperiously, "have you satisfied yourself that the man was strangled?"

"Yeah. It wasn't a rope. But it should have been."

"What do you mean?" asked Carrie.

Gunn stepped away from the body, looked at them. Lamplight flickered over his face, hardened the contours of his high cheekbones, the strong jawline, threw shadows into his pale blue-gray eyes.

"Man dies that quick it's usually through a trapdoor.

46

At the end of a rope. His neck is broken, but he wasn't hanged. He wasn't drug through the brush. Mighty peculiar."

"Peculiar?" asked Winifred, her voice rising in pitch.

Gunn heaved a sigh. The woman was positively morbid. He supposed she needed to know since she hadn't actually seen her husband that way, but Carrie might have. He looked at her, to see if she could take it. Her eyes blinked and she nodded her approval. As if she knew, beforehand, what he was going to say.

"This man was strangled. By someone with powerful hands."

The women shuddered simultaneously.

Carrie stared at Gunn transfixed as if reliving the memory of her own husband's death. Winifred's eyes misted.

Serena drew herself up, stared into the night with a hard look.

Pablo crossed himself.

"El Guante," he whispered, but no one heard him.

"Let's all go inside," said Carrie, finally. "Pablo, will you see to it that Mister Wallen is taken to a quiet comfortable place."

"And saddle our horses," said Serena. "We'll go to Sally's tonight, Carrie, and on to Palomas from there."

"But you can't. . . ." protested Carrie.

"No, my daughter is right," said Winifred. "We must see to Mrs. Wallen, extend a hand of comfort to her in this terrible hour."

Carrie said nothing.

"I'll ride with you, ladies," said Gunn.

Winifred, who had started toward the house, stopped, whirled on Gunn.

47

"That won't be necessary," she said. "We know our way."

Gunn felt a hand on his arm. Carrie squeezed it with urgent fingers. He looked down at her as she shook her head.

Winifred entered the house. Carrie held Gunn back. Serena, following her mother, seemed about to go inside, but stopped, lingering.

Gunn and Carrie walked up to her, stopped, waiting to hear what she had to say.

"Now that you've seen for yourself what my mother was trying to tell you, I suppose you'll be on your way, Gunn."

Gunn's heart pounded in his chest. Serena's expression was noncommital, but her beauty shone through, even in the dark. This wasn't his fight. He didn't know these people. Yet he had never seen a man so brutally slain, so heartlessly murdered. A strong man, a very powerful man, had put his hands on Mort Wallen's throat and squeezed until the breath was gone. Then, with a mighty wrench, he had broken the man's neck. Or, maybe he had done it all at once. The windpipe was crushed; squashed like an eggshell. Any man who could do that would be unusual. He might even stand out in a crowd. Such a man would have mighty hands and muscular shoulders. His fingers would be extremely strong. It could be a man like Paddy Ryan. Whoever, wherever, such a man was, someone would know what he could do with those hands. Such a man could not hide his strength nor his tendency to kill by strangulation for very long. Such a man could be found.

"Why no, ma'am," Gunn said. "I reckon I'll stay on a while. See what I can find out."

48

Serena's face didn't alter its expression.

"May I ask your reasons? Why the sudden decision to change your mind?"

"That man had a wife, kids. He was in the prime of life. I don't like to see a man die like that."

"No," she said. "It's a horrible way to die."

Gunn heard Serena sobbing to herself as she turned and disappeared into the house.

"I should go with them," he said to Carrie.

"No," she said. "Leave them be. You can stay the night, then decide what you should do in the morning."

"I don't get it, Carrie. Do you ladies want me to help or not?"

"Let them work out their grief in their own way. I know how they feel. Being with Sally will help them. They will have something to share. Winifred and Serena will find the right words to say. Your presence would be . . . awkward."

"I see," he said.

Gunn knew what grief was. Raw gray grease grief like a sliding oil over the senses. Like a pall over the landscape of the soul. Like a strangling shroud. When Laurie, his wife, had died, he had worked out his grief in his own way. Avenged her death. Tracked down the men responsible, one by one, and given them eternity with a bucking pistol in his hand. When someone you loved died, you were alone. Words didn't help much. There was no comfort, either, in vengeance. That course had led him down strange trails and when he came to the end of it he was shocked, stunned by the reality of what had happened to Laurie. Oh, the men had been part of it, but the actual murder was a senseless, stupid, unnecessary thing—like that man Mort Wallen's had been.

Could men kill over land? Over a piece of dirt? Gunn knew they could. Such things had been done before, would be done again.

He really had no business mixing into this. But Winifred and Serena had laid down a challenge. And now he had come bluntfaced up to their problems. He had seen death's face in another guise, in the dead face of a stranger. And if he did not stop to help, who would? Was he his brother's keeper? Maybe. Maybe not. But if no one called Mort's killer to answer, then what good was life? Perhaps Mort had not known who his killer was. Perhaps it was time to find the widowmaker and call him out, cut off those deadly hands so that he could kill no more.

"Gunn, do you really want to stay and help? Could you? Would you?"

"I'll stay."

"If it's a question of money. . . ."

"It's not. It's a question of who I am. . . ."

His voice trailed off and he took Carrie's arm, led her back into the house. It was quiet in the living room after Carrie left him to see to her guests. He fished in his pockets for the makings, built himself a cigarette. He struck a match, felt the warmth flare against his face. He pulled the smoke deep into his lungs, found an ashtray handy on a table, sat down to wait for Serena and her mother.

He stood up, after a while, finished his cigarette by the window at the far end of the room. Looking out, he could see the lights of El Paso in the distance. A sound startled him and he turned away from the window, the cigarette a glowing stub in his fingers.

"They've gone," said Carrie, entering the room.

"Gone?"

"Serena and her mother left by the back way."

Gunn was disappointed. He had wanted to see Serena again. Look into her eyes. Reassure her. Hear her talk one more time.

"Aren't you worried?"

"No," said Carrie. "Pablo's going with them. Serena is armed and Winifred can shoot rather well."

Gunn found the ashtray again, put out his cigarette. It had burnt his fingers, but he ignored the pain.

"I'm sorry the evening was spoiled," she said. "Would you like to retire now?"

"Yes, if you don't mind. I'd like to ride up to Palomas early."

She smiled weakly at him, kept her distance as if realizing that they were alone in the big house.

"You might find some suspicion when you go there," she said. "After all that has happened. I'll tell you how to get to Serena's, and she can vouch for you."

"Do you ever go there?"

"Not much. I—I've always liked the city. We built our home here so that I could see El Paso from the window. Luna Creek is wild, untamed. My husband loved it, but he compromised. For my sake."

"I see."

Carrie led him down a hallway, opened a door in the middle. A lamp flickered on a table. The room reeked of perfume.

Gunn's eyebrows went up.

"Serena's room. When she stays here. I thought it would be better since she isn't here. I could make up another room if you don't like it."

"It will do. Thanks, Carrie."

"Good night. I'm in the master bedroom at the end of the hall. If you need anything."

Before he could say anything, she was gone. He closed the door, listened to her footsteps on the hardwood floor.

He undressed quickly, climbed into bed. The bed was soft, the sheets fresh linen. But the room still retained the scent of Serena. A delicate fragrance that reminded him of her. He leaned over, reached for the lamp. He turned the wick down, lifted the chimney and blew out the flame. The chimney clattered back into its seat.

It was quiet and the night dark as pitch through the windows.

The tooth hurt like hell.

It hadn't bothered him much earlier that evening, but now it was a throbbing spear in his gums.

He touched the tooth. It wiggled between his fingers.

An intense pain shot up the nerve ends. He didn't touch it anymore. But, the tooth would have to go. It was an upper tooth, the fourth from the center. He'd go to a blacksmith shop and wangle a pair of pliers, drink some whiskey and pull it himself.

Gunn put the throbbing tooth out of his mind. The pain gradually subsided as the nerve ends dulled now that he wasn't worrying the loose tooth with his tongue or fingers.

He was drifting off to sleep when the shattering of glass reached his ears.

Gunn shot up straight, leaped out of bed. Grabbing his trousers, he slipped them on over bare skin, hobbled to the door. He felt his way across the room, out into the hall.

The sound had come from the front. Probably the living room.

Cursing, he went back inside the bedroom, fumbled for a sulphur match in his vest. Finding one, he groped his way to the lamp on the bedside table. He struck the match on the table leg. It flared into being and he found the turning nob on the wick. Lifted the chimney and touched the match to the oil-soaked wick. The lamp smoked, then glowed as he adjusted the wick.

A flicker of light danced in the hallway as Gunn turned back toward the door. He jerked his pistol from its holster, held it ready.

"Gunn? Was that you?"

"No," he said, going through the door. Carrie stood there with a lamp in her hand, holding it by a curved handle. The lamp had a reflector on it, threw a lot of light. "Something broke a window."

"I—I wasn't asleep, but I'm frightened now."

"Stay here if you want." Gunn started down the hall, the lamp wobbling in his left hand. He held his pistol up, his thumb on the hammer.

"I—I'm too scared to stay here alone," said Carrie, running after him, her slippers whispering over the hardwood. She looked at Gunn's broad bare back, the giant shadow of his form thrown on the wall by the lamp in her hand. It was reassuring to see his muscles rippling under his flesh, see the pistol in his hand.

Gunn saw the reason for the noise.

The window pane by the door was shattered. Glass shards and splinters lay strewn on the floor and rug next to the coat-tree. A large stone with a paper tied around it lay amidst a few splinters of glass.

Someone had entered the patio on foot, hurled the stone and then run away. Or else was still out there.

"Stay here," Gunn said, setting the lamp on a table.

"Where are you going?"

"Outside."

He slipped out the door, closed it quickly. He waited until his eyes became accustomed to the darkness. Then, he walked barefooted across the patio, cocking his pistol. The flagstones were cold on his feet. He stopped, listened.

Beyond the arch, he saw nothing.

Whoever had been there, was gone. In the morning, he could check the tracks. If there were any.

Back inside, he saw Carrie stooping down, the paper in her hands. The string lay on the floor next to the rock. Gunn eased the hammer down on his pistol.

"What is it?" he asked.

"I—I think this was meant for you." She handed Gunn the paper. It was ordinary butcher paper. The handwriting was crude, with block lettering.

STRANGER YOU GOT NO BIZNESS HERE. GET OUT! STAY AWAY FROM PALOMAS.

There was no signature. Gunn hadn't expected any.

"They—they know you're here, Gunn."

"Yeah. I reckon."

Someone must have followed him there, or seen him ride away from town, following Carrie and Pablo.

Carrie stood up, looked into Gunn's gray slate eyes. Impulsively, she put her arms around his naked waist. Squeezed him.

He felt her body shudder against his.

"Gunn," she breathed, "I'm scared. Real scared. It reminds me of . . . of something I've tried to forget."

"I know."

"They did the same thing warning my husband. Before . . . before they murdered him."

"Don't worry," he said. "They've already proved something to me. Twice."

"What's that?" Her voice quavered with fear.

"They're cowards."

He put his arms around her. For the first time he noticed how sheer her nightgown was. He could see her flesh, feel it warm against his own.

"Hold me," she breathed. "Just keep holding me, Gunn."

CHAPTER SIX

Gunn's loins swarmed with heat.

Carrie's body pulsed against his. Her flesh warm under the transparent cloth of her gown. Her breasts mashed against his bare chest made his flesh tingle.

"Will you come to my bed?" she asked.

He smelled her hair, tilted her face up to his. Looked into her swimming eyes, eyes that were watery with emotion.

"Yes, if you want me to."

"I want you, Gunn. You're the only man to come into this house since my husband died. I—I never knew how awful my loneliness was until this minute."

"No need to explain, Carrie. I know."

"Yes, you do, don't you? I sensed that. Gunn, I want you so bad I can't stand it. I don't know what you'll think of me, but I don't care."

He put a finger to her lips, released his grip on her.

"Come on," he said. "Before you change your mind."

The note fluttered to the floor, forgotten. Gunn carried his own lamp, followed Carrie, with her lamp, to her bedroom. Her buttocks bounced provocatively before him, visible under the sheer fabric of her nightgown. Her sandals shuffled on the hardwood as he padded along behind her, his desire even stronger than before.

Carrie set the door latch and took the lamp from his hands. She set both lamps on her dresser, blew out one. Gunn stood there, surveying the room. It was wide, comfortable, with a large wooden bed, a dresser, a pair of wardrobes, a desk, chairs, a table, night tables. It was a man's room, but also a woman's. There were flowers in a vase, rifles on the walls. A fireplace, a few pictures. A bear rug and a couple of deerskin rugs graced the polished hardwood floors. Carrie stood before the mirror, facing Gunn. She could not see her reflection, but he could, and she looked beautiful from both angles. Very beautiful. Her lips pursed and she beckoned to him.

"Kiss me," she said.

Gunn went to her, took her in his arms.

He kissed her on the lips. Her response was a shy murmur and she seemed stiff with fear.

"God, it's been so long," she breathed.

"Are you afraid?"

"A little."

"Of me?"

"Of myself. I was a good wife, Gunn. I never looked at another man."

He held her close to him, rubbed the back of her neck. She was tense, the muscles hard. She put her hand on his arm, rubbed the bare muscles, traced delicate fingers over the hard bone of his shoulder. Touched his hair. He felt desire rising in him. Blood surged into his manhood, propelling it outward so that his hardness touched her leg. She winced, but she did not move away.

He kissed her again. This time, he moved his lips

against hers, mashing them, exerting pressure. His tongue slipped inside her mouth, into the wetness. Her tongue touched his and he felt her body jolt against his. Her loins pressed against his leg. She began rubbing her sex back and forth, then up and down. His cock hardened even more and the first seepings of fluid began oozing from its tip. His pants were tautened by the growing stalk between his legs. Carrie shifted her position and rubbed against the swelling bone. He felt the softness of her beneath the thin cloth.

He wanted her.

"Take me," she husked. "I don't care what it looks like. Just take me, Gunn."

"Yes," he said quietly, stepping away. He stripped out of his trousers, let them fall to the floor.

She stared at him, her eyes widening.

"You're so—so big," she whispered.

Gunn stepped up to her, slid the straps from her shoulders. Her gown dripped to the floor. She was naked beneath it. He slid his cock between her legs, pushed upward so that its length nudged the lips of her sex-cleft. Then he kissed her again as he bent his knees. He lowered himself, moved his buttocks backwards. His manhood slid along the crease. She spread her legs slightly and he pushed upward, sliding into her sheath.

Carrie gasped as he entered her.

Then Gunn grasped her buttocks, lifted her in the air, held her like a rocking chair. He slid her up and down on his shaft as her arms encircled his neck. He buried his swollen member in the moist hot recesses of her honeyed folds. She was light, featherlight, and he lifted her up and down easily, sliding his cock in and out as she began to tremble and shudder.

In and out, he plumbed her.

Carrie shook as the first orgasm rippled through her loins.

She opened her mouth in a gasping sigh. Her fingers dug into his shoulders. He let her sink to the hilt of his stalk. She bucked with a sudden smashing climax. He brought her up again, let her sink slowly down on his impaling spear.

And, again, Carrie spasmed.

He held her there until her shudders subsided, then lifted her off. He carried her to the bed as she clung to him, weak, tears glistening in her eyes. She looked up at him in awe, like a child. The reflector lamp threw their shadows against the wall.

He lay her gently on the bed, climbed in beside her.

"Are you still afraid?" he asked. "Did I hurt you?"

"No, no, no, no," she said. "I never knew it could be like that. So quick. So beautiful." She paused, looking into his shadowy eyes. "So natural."

He touched a breast with his finger.

Teased the nipple. He swirled the tip with his finger until it hardened like chinquapin. Then he bent down and kissed the same nipple, squeezed it with his lips. Slid his tongue on its flat rubbery tip, over the rough sponginess of it until she quivered all over as if a feather had been brushed up and down her back.

He kissed the other breast, worrying the nipple in his mouth, grazing it with his teeth.

And her hand found him, grasped the sex-slick shaft and squeezed the choked veins, the blood-hardened flesh.

She stroked his cock up and down very slowly. Raging sensations flooded his loins. He swallowed half of her breast, soaking the hardened nipple in hot saliva.

Carrie squirmed with desire.

"I want it again," she husked. "Inside me."

It was time. If she stroked him any more he would spill his seed in her hand. He lifted his head, looked into her eyes, lambent with lamplight. She was ready. More than ready. He could almost hear her purring. She released her hold on his manhood. Spread her legs wide to receive him.

"Hurry, Gunn, hurry."

He rose above her, dipped to enter her.

His swollen cock touched the sensitive crease of her vagina. Carrie's body leaped as if galvanized. He slid through the portals into her steam-hot sheath, burrowed through the pulsing folds of flesh, skewering her wriggling hips to the mattress.

Carrie bucked with a sudden orgasm.

Her soft body turned hard with desire. As Gunn bored into her, she undulated like a dancer, smacked her loins into his with steely fury. He drove deep and she made him go deeper. Each thrust of his cock was met with an upward thrust of hers. Loin to loin, they danced to primitive rhythms. Thigh to thigh, they met in mortal combat, naked as Eden savages encountering love for the first time.

Gunn was surprised at Carrie's energy. The more he drove into her, the harder she rose up to impale herself. He felt the strength in her legs, her hips.

She did unbelievable things with her muscles.

Squeezing him, releasing him. Contracting, expanding.

All of her pent-up feelings seemed to boil up inside her, rush over the brim to engulf him.

She was heat and light, silk and savagery, pagan and

wanton and lusty all at once. Only her eyes, shimmering with wetness and amber lampglow told him how vulnerable she was, how naked of soul. But her body was an unleashed animal, grinding against his with a furious lust that asked for everything he could give her—and more.

"Gunn, Gunn, Gunn. . . ." she sobbed, thrashing upward with powerful pushes, her feet flat, her legs widespread, her arms around his neck.

But he matched her urgent upthrusts with powerful downthrusts of his own.

Slammed into her with hard-bone loins, ramming deep with his battering manhood as if to tear through her, sip at a hidden spring buried beyond her womb. She took all of him and begged for more. Begged with her wet mouth and her moist eyes, with her wild thighs, her eager legs. Begged him with the oils of her sex and the might of her loins.

"More," she said, senselessly.

And he gave her more when there was no more left. More.

And still more.

Until he was desperate to satisfy her. Until she was screaming softly in his ears and clawing his back and wrenching his neck until it threatened to break in half like a matchstick. Until he was racing with her, mindless in the half-dark, crazy in the amber glow of the room, senseless in the rocking tempo of sex that triggered forgotten muscles, drew him along the wild pounding path that climbed upward to dizzying heights beyond the senses, beyond feeling itself.

She was a ragdoll slamming into him, an out-of-control animal thrashing in its death-throes. Climaxing in concatenous bursts like a string of Chinese firecrackers going off as the fuse burned and burned with a hissing deadly urgency that sizzled like angry bees.

Gunn held on. Somehow.

He rode the whirlwind. Stayed on the bucking mare like a man tied to the stirrups, strapped to the saddle. Hung on and hunkered deeper until she stopped screaming and her strength ebbed like a tide after a storm. Hung on until she begged him to finish it, to kill the snake in his loins, to douse the awesome fires that raged through her like a wind-whipped conflagration in dry timber.

"Now!" he yelled, holding onto her loins, pressing her body tightly against his as if to fuse them into one being.

"Yes, oh yes, Gunn, now!" she screamed, her fingernails raking his back, digging through the flesh, spurting blood from his torn skin.

Seed burst from his seminal vesicles, spurted into her in a milky rush.

Gunn quivered in climax, the tip of his manhood as tender as an eyeball.

Let his weight sag against her. Floated there, lost, empty, sated, full as a man could be with nothing left of his power.

Lay there atop her, his lungs burning, sucking in breath like a man saved from drowning.

Lay there at peace, her arms around him, her soft breasts mashed under the weight of his chest.

Carrie breathing hard, her eyes closed, her mouth open wide.

"I'm so full of you," she said, a few moments later. She squeezed him with a loving tenderness, then released him with the last of her strength. "So grateful to you, Gunn.

For this, for giving me back myself."

He rolled from her body onto his back.

"It was good, Carrie," he said.

"I know. I'm amazed."

Gunn said nothing. He looked up at the log beams of the ceiling and let his muscles fall back into place. Muscles that had been wrenched into strings of sinew, into threads of tendons. He let his mind drift like a balloon unleashed from its mooring.

"He's gone," Carrie said, after a long silence.

Gunn felt the balloon sink, leaden, back to earth.

He shook his head to clear it. The shock of coming back down was jolting. Down from wherever he had been.

"Huh? Who's gone?"

Carrie laughed. A dry thin laugh like corn husks rattling in a wind.

"I'm sorry," she said. "I—I was just listening to the house breathe. And to you. But, he's gone. Thanks to you."

Gunn felt a shivery chill brush against the hackles of his neck.

"I don't savvy," he said, drifting into the vernacular.

"Do you want to smoke? I can bring you tobacco, papers. Eugene always smoked afterwards."

Gunn remembered. Eugene was her husband. Had been. But he was dead. Murdered by the strangler. Like Mort Wallen. Like Anthony Paxton.

"No," he said. "I don't want to smoke."

Carrie laughed again. Her hand touched his arm.

"I'm being silly. If I tell you something, will you promise not to make fun of me."

"I promise."

"Ever since Eugene died, was killed, I've been

63

haunted. This house has been haunted. No, not really, I suppose. But I felt his presence. Or thought I did. Sometimes I would hear him in the next room, talking. Or I'd come into the living room and smell the smoke from his tobacco. At night, well, at night it was the worst. I'd hear footsteps, the rustle of cloth. That voice of his humming one of those old songs he used to sing sometimes. But it must have been my imagination, I know."

"When you cherish someone real deep you can imagine they're still alive after they're gone."

"I know. I used to see Eugene in town, or sitting out on the patio, but it was only shadows, or someone who resembled him. But tonight, it's quiet in the house. No footsteps. No singing. And I don't smell his tobacco. I feel, well, relieved. And happy. Very happy."

"I hope he hasn't gone away on my account," Gunn said uneasily.

"No, don't think that! It's just that I feel alive. As if I've been reborn. It was very good, Gunn. The best I've ever had. I want you to know that."

"Thank you."

He was silent for awhile, then he heard singing. Humming, really. He looked down, crooking his neck to see, and Carrie was murmuring a melody he had long forgotten.

"Two Little Boys Were Going to School," he said.

"What?"

"That's the name of that song you're humming."

"Is it? I never knew. Do you know the words?"

"There's a lot of different versions. I know one."

"Will you sing them to me some time?"

"Maybe."

His tooth had started to throb again. Carrie stopped humming. She got up, blew out the lamp. He felt her crawl back into bed, snuggled against him. He closed his eyes, put his arm around her, drawing her close.

It was nice to sleep with a woman again.

It was nice to forget about tomorrow for a little while.

Life was better than death any day.

"Good night, Gunn."

"Good night."

They slept and the house went silent.

There were no ghosts. Only darkness and the breathing of dreamers.

CHAPTER SEVEN

It should have taken Gunn no more than two hours to reach Palomas.

Instead, it looked as if he might not reach it at all.

He had lingered in bed with Carrie. Then over breakfast. Before he left she had begged him not to go. She read the note again and decided that it was too dangerous.

Poor Carrie.

Her eyes were filled with love for him and now she wanted him to move right in, add his horse to her remuda. But he knew it wouldn't work. Not with the "troubles" hanging over them.

Not with the threat delivered the night before.

Probably by the same men who had killed Mort Wallen. The same ones who had murdered Paxton and Roberts.

How many more would die until Torreon gave up on his attempt to grab the land along Luna Creek?

Maybe a few more now that Gunn knew he had been followed and that at least two men were closing the gap.

He'd had the odd feeling that all was not right ever since saddling up Duke and kissing Carrie goodbye.

Looking out over the flat land below the slope he had seen nothing. But there was that hitch between his shoulder blades, that flutter of moths in his gut that told him there was more than lizards and saguaro out there.

Now, he knew for sure.

They were well back, at first. He had spotted one when he turned quickly, saw a quick flash of something bright. Not a rifle or a pistol barrel, but something small. Like a button. Or the rowels on a spur.

The hunch working still.

Then, the other one had appeared as a black speck of movement, cutting across his backtrail looking for cover. Just a quick glimpse. But enough to Gunn's trained and wary eye.

Whoever had written that warning note had meant business.

Whoever was following him was some careless.

And that bothered him.

Maybe they wanted to press him. Keep him headed toward Palomas. Toward an ambush.

Could be.

If so, his destiny lay up ahead and not very far. The two men were closing the distance gradually. One on his right, the other on his left. He saw them each out of a corner of his eye every so often. As they topped a rise over ground he had already covered. Making no effort to slip through the gullies and arroyos to catch him by surprise.

So maybe someone was waiting for him ahead.

Along Luna Creek. Behind a cottonwood. Standing next to a saguaro. Lying flat in an arroyo ready to spring up Apache-style and blow him out of the saddle.

Guess again.

Gunn had stayed well above the creek, keeping to high ground. The creek went underground every so often, but now it was running on the surface, cutting a wide swath through steep banks. Beyond, the gully twisted and the creek disappeared from view. The country was broken, criss-crossed with arroyos, ditches, gullies, *vados*.

If it was going to happen, it would happen there.

He would be out in the open some of the time and an ambusher could take him easily from a number of concealed positions.

Gunn dug blunt spurs into Duke's flanks, laid the rein on the horse's neck to turn him without pulling on the bit. Duke switched his tail and moved back on a line leading east to El Paso. Gunn rode the high ground long enough for his trackers to see him, then cut down into the arroyo where the creek flowed underground.

Then, he kicked Duke into a fast gallop.

Duke took the path of least resistance as Gunn gave the animal his head. The sun was up over the hills and the mist had burned off so that the air was turning warm. It was still a good morning to run. Duke ran, putting distance between Gunn and his pursuers.

The creek rose again abruptly, breaking through the earth on hard rock. Gunn swung to the south, cutting up through an arroyo that had been carved out of the earth by centuries of flash floods. This time of year it was bone dry and Duke had to zigzag to avoid rocks that had become lodged here and there. The arroyo petered out.

Gunn debated on whether to stay there and wait or circle, try to double back on the men who followed him. If he rode up out of the arroyo, he would expose himself. But if he stayed there, he'd be in a box.

Duke blew, but the horse was not seriously winded.

Gunn made his choice.

"Up, boy, up!" he said, gently raking the spurs into Duke's flanks. The horse scrambled up the slope of the arroyo, powerful hind legs digging in and hooves driving so that they topped the cactus-lined wall easily.

There was no sign of the men who were following him.

Gunn kept to the open, using only the saguaro for cover. If either man came for him it would have to be across flat or gently rolling ground. And he would see them in time to break out the Winchester, draw a bead.

He kept his eyes ranging up and down the arroyo.

He kicked Duke into a hard trot.

Something was wrong. He neither saw anyone nor heard anything. Had the men followed him down the arroyo? That would be likely.

A muscle began to twitch in Gunn's jaw as his mouth tightened in a frown. His tooth sent shoots of pain through his gums.

"Whoa boy," he said to Duke, pulling the reins up against his chest with his left hand.

The horse slowed, stopped, and settled down. Snorted.

Gunn strained to hear.

A pair of doves flushed below him and his right hand darted toward his pistol. Three crows chased a squealing hawk, attacking from the rear. Gunn watched them fly over the horizon.

It was dead quiet.

Almost.

A hissing sound filled the air.

Gunn twisted in the saddle, saw the rope whispering toward him. His nerves danced as ice water rippled down his spine. Out of the corner of his eye he saw the man, leaning over his saddle, by a saguaro.

The rope swirled over his shoulders, dropped fast.

Thinking quickly, he shot his right arm straight up.

The manila rope pulled tight around his waist. He felt a searing pain under his right armpit. His left arm was pinned.

He felt a jerk and saw the ground rush up to meet him.

With a wild yell, the man on horseback wrapped the rope around his saddle horn. The horse, a claybank, backed hard. The man kicked the horse, reined him full circle.

Gunn felt the rope tighten, then pull him.

He knew he had to act fast, before the horse took off. He had landed on his left side. A wracking pain in his left arm was now replaced by a stunning numbness. Quickly, he reached for his knife as he started to move. In seconds, he would be dragged through cactus, over rock. He'd be pulp before he'd gone a quarter mile.

The knife came free. Gunn's hand clasped around it, just under the eagle's head.

With a mighty effort, he swung his arm around, slashed at the rope. The blade struck it, slid off.

Gunn twisted as the horse on the other end of the rope gained speed. He bounced over onto his back. Rocks and sand smashed against his flesh. He struggled to strike the rope again.

The man on horseback was going up hill. A point in Gunn's favor. But the horse was gaining more speed. Gunn started to yaw back and forth, making it harder for him to slash at the rope.

His left arm was useless, pinned tight by the rope.

Faster and faster, Gunn went, jerked over the rough ground. He managed to get his right arm under the rope. He stretched straight back, felt the rope bounce against the knife blade. He left it there and sawed back and forth.

The strands began to part. He pushed up, exerting more pressure on the blade.

"I got him, Barney!" yelled Alfie Sloan.

Gunn heard a muffled reply from somewhere off to his left.

So, there were at least two men. Maybe there hadn't been a third. If his luck held. Or changed. So far it had been all bad. One of the men must have managed to sneak up behind him, wait until he passed near. The claybank had blended perfectly into the terrain and the man had the advantage of the sun at his back. Gunn just plain hadn't seen him.

The rope strands parted rapidly now.

Gunn couldn't wait. He was bouncing hard and only this had prevented his head from being ground to mash by the gravelly earth. Miraculously, it stayed on. He pushed hard and the sharp blade cut through the remaining strands of manila.

Gunn skidded to a stop.

"He's loose, Alfie!" came a shout.

Gunn knew he had only seconds to save himself.

He loosened the rope as he stood up, crouching. He rammed the knife back in its sheath, snatched at the butt of his Colt .45.

Alfie, on the claybank, stood up in the stirrups as he reined in his horse. He saw Gunn, reached for his rifle.

It was a mistake.

Gunn hammered back, squeezed. The Colt bucked in his hand. Alfie threw up his arms, tumbled out of the saddle.

Moans reached Gunn's ears.

But he had no time to check on Alfie.

The other rider came fast, over the rise. He had his pistol out, was firing straight at Gunn.

71

Bullets spanged on the rocks, spat grit and stone at Gunn.

Gunn couldn't see the man's face, nor much of his body. He had no clear shot, but if he didn't act fast the man would run him down or ride right over him.

Behind him, Alfie sat up, a spreading stain of red across the belly part of his shirt. He clawed his pistol free, aimed at Gunn through diming eyes. Fired.

Gunn heard the explosion, felt the bullet whiz past his face. Eight inches.

Still, Barney came on, leaning over the side of his horse, firing from under the mane.

"Shit!" said Gunn, disgusted.

There was nothing to do, but kill an innocent animal.

A bullet plowed through the saguaro two feet in front of him.

Gunn dashed to one side, gripped the Colt with two hands. He found the horse's heart, tracked it, squeezed.

The bullet smashed the horse just behind its left foreleg. Found the heart, burst it like a balloon. The horse dropped like an arrow-shot deer. Barney sailed on, over its head.

Gunn cocked fast, waited until Barney hit. As the man struggled to rise, he shot him in the temple. The range was less than fifteen yards. The man's head exploded like a melon, spraying blood and brains in a semi-arc. Barney crumpled over, dead before his torso hit the ground.

Gunn whirled toward Alfie.

Alfie sat there, his face drained of color. The pistol wavered in his hand.

Thirty yards away.

Gunn looked at him.

Alfie seemed to be trying to decide whether to shoot again or not.

"Pull it and it'll be the last thing you do," said Gunn.

"God, man, is Barney dead?"

"As a stone."

The pistol tumbled from Alfie's hand. He clutched his belly, rocked there on his haunches.

Gunn approached him warily.

Full of pain. The tooth ramming up to his brain like a spiny locust thorn. Back like a flayed piece of meat. Head throbbing like a hammer-hit thumb. Legs aching, shoulders weighing down on him as if he carried an ore-car full on his back.

In no mood to bargain.

Mad as hell and then some.

Alfie sat there, shivering, with a glazed look in his eyes. Shiny eyes like an animal's when it's sore wounded in a trap and has gnawed through half of its leg and sees the hunter come up for the final cut with the knife.

Jesus, he looked bad.

Real bad.

Gunn's shadow fell across the wounded man.

Alfie looked up at the broad-shouldered man with the slate eyes and a calm came over him. Dry-mouthed, he licked parched lips.

"How many of you?"

Alfie winced as some new pain echoed through his body like a stone thrown down a deep dark shaft.

"Two."

"You and what's his name? Bernie?"

"Barney Houlihan. Man, I'm fair gut-shot and you're standin' there all primed like death itself."

"I remember you from town. El Paso. You work for Torreon?"

"Uuunnh."

"Whereabouts are the others? That Paddy feller?"

"Me and Paddy, we work for him, and Jack, Barney. Good God, man, are you just going to stand there throwin' your shadow over me while my blood leaks out?"

Gunn looked at Alfie closely. The feverish lips, the crimson stain circular on his shirt belly-high, the beads of sweat on his forehead, just above his lips. It was hell watching a man go like that. Scared. Scared of the dark that would come soon. Scared of the emptiness that was bound to happen.

"I can pack you into Palomas."

Alfie's eyes went wide. Fear. Pure fear. Like a chicken bone in the throat. Like a band around the chest. An iron band that kept tightening, tightening.

"I—I couldn't make it. You got any whiskey?"

Gunn shook his head.

"I'm pure hurt inside. Feels like a big rock in there." Alfie looked down and saw all the thick blood on his hand. The hole was flowing blood. No pumping like an artery, just sliding out of him, smelling like slit intestines. Like something the flies would feed on as soon as they got the scent.

"What about this Torreon?" Gunn asked. "How much he pay you for my hide?"

"Hunnert dollars. Me and Barney."

"I must not be worth much."

"He—he, Torreon, he's just some *caballero* what lives in Juarez, wants this land out here. I don't like him much, but it's been hard scrabble 'till we hooked up with him."

"You Irish?"

"Nope. Tennessee."

Alfie laid back on his hips, suddenly tired. His eyes flickered with light. The sweat slicked his forehead, dripped into his eyes. He blinked. He made some soft gasping sounds. He looked even more tired than before.

"You got family?"

Alfie shook his head. A little bit. His eyes closed, then opened. Wide.

"They don't give a damn. Ma's alive. Pa dead at Chickamauga. Sisters scattered."

"You picked a hard trail, man."

"I thought you was easy. You got a name? I don't even know your name. . . ." Alfie's words were slurred. Tired. Slow words punched out from a throat that was tightening up with an agony deep inside him.

"They call me Gunn."

"Gunn? What kind of name is that?"

"Just a name."

"My name's Horace Alfred Sloan. I was named after that newspaper man."

"The one who told all the young men to go west?"

"Yeah. That's the one."

"Too bad," said Gunn. "Too many of your kind came out here. For all the wrong reasons."

"I—I got kin," said Horace Alfred Sloan, "back home in Tennessee."

Gunn stiffened as Alfie lay down as if resting and closed his eyes.

Gunn hammered down, shoved the Colt in its holster.

He looked at the face of the dying man. He wanted to tell him that he probably wasn't named after Greeley, but after a Roman poet who lived centuries before. Alfie was too old to have been named for the newspaperman. It didn't matter. Except that Gunn didn't want to kill a boy. Alfie was a man, probably in his early twenties.

Alfie's face twitched, then the muscles sagged.

In seconds, he was dead.

CHAPTER EIGHT

Gunn caught up the claybank, gentled it down. He hefted Alfie's body up on the saddle, belly down. He tied his stiffening legs to the stirrup on one side; tied his arms to the stirrup on the opposite side. He led the horse over to where the body of Barney Houlihan lay. He looked at the brands on both horses. A Diamond T. He didn't have to disturb the dead horse, Barney's. The brand was plain on its left hip. As it was on the claybank gelding's.

Barney's face had no shape anymore. One side of his head was gone.

The tall, gray-eyed man slid Barney up beside Alfie, stretching him belly down in back of the cantle. He cut the reins from the bridle on the dead horse, used these to tie Barney's legs and arms to Alfie's. Satisfied, he led the claybank downslope toward where he hoped Duke would be waiting.

The big dun nickered, waited as Gunn strode up to him. Duke eyed the claybank with its mortal cargo, but did not shy.

Gunn caught him up, mounted in one flowing motion, pain stretching through flesh and bone.

He rode toward Palomas. That was the place to take the

dead men. Torreon's men. Not to El Paso, where questions would be asked, snipers alerted. Palomas. That was where Torreon had struck and where he would meet his defeat. It was also where Serena Paxton was. And Serena, despite his night with Carrie, was the woman Gunn wanted.

****

Palomas loomed up on the shimmering landscape, a small, cluttered, closely-packed hodgepodge of adobes, false fronts and scattered huts smack on the bank of Luna Creek.

Gunn rode down to the wide dusty road, passed the sign that said *Welcome to Palomas, Pop. 38*. The sign was weathered, cracked. It sagged on its post and a good wind would probably blow it down soon.

People stared at the tall man on the dun leading a horse loaded with two dead men.

The talk spread up the main street and men started coming to the door of the saloon. Gunn stopped there, looked up at the false front. The sign said JIMBO'S EMPORIUM in huge painted-on letters that curved across the weathered wood in red and green. Hideous.

One of the men stepped through the bat-wing doors, onto the dusty street.

"Don't haul no garbage into Palomas, stranger," he said to Gunn. "'Pears to me that claybank's stamped with a Diamond T."

"It is. You recognize either jasper laid across its back?"

"One of 'em. Trash."

"Exactly," said Gunn, swinging down from the saddle.

77

"And it's your garbage, feller. I'm just the delivery man."

"That so?"

The man bent his knees, leaned slightly backward. One hand floated near the butt of his pistol. He was bowlegged, short, with a face cracked and stained by the wind and sun of New Mexico. His dark brown eyes squinted at Gunn, looking for any sign of hostility.

"One of 'em mentioned Palomas before he died. That one on the saddle there. Called himself Alfie."

A burly man with a hawk feather streaming from his hatband muscled his way through the throng of men crowding the entrance to the saloon.

It was then that Gunn noticed something he had missed before. Every man jack he saw had a black crepe band on his arm. He looked at some of the windows out of the corner of his eye and saw that these too, were hung with crepe.

Palomas was in mourning!

"What's going on out here?" asked the burly man, who stood a head taller than the others. "Did you say Alfie was dead? Alfie Sloan?"

The men outside parted so that the big man with the feather in his hat had elbow room.

"That's Sloan over the saddle," said Gunn.

"And who in Billy Hell are you?"

"The name's Gunn."

"Well, Gunn, we're having a wake for a friend of ours. And we have a place for that wolf meat on that claybank gelding. If you're a drinking man, come on into Jimbo's Emporium and wet your whistle. If not, piss on you!"

Gunn laughed. A hearty laugh that boomed out of his chest.

"Are you Jimbo?"

"Jim Bobbitt. They call me Jimbo. They call me Big Jim. They call me late for super, too."

Gunn stepped forward, twirled his reins around the hitchrail. Bobbitt thrust out a hand that looked as if it could crush rock. Gunn took it, squeezed hard to keep from losing at least three of his fingers.

The two men sized up one another. Gunn was impressed with Jimbo's direct gaze, his bluff manner. He smelled the whiskey on his breath, but Jimbo's eyes were clear, hard as agate.

"I'll drink with you, Jimbo. I didn't know Wallen, but I saw what happened to him."

"You must have been at Mrs. Roberts."

"I was and I'm buyin' in, at her request."

"We sent some men to fetch Wallen, bring him here for decent buryin'. When they get back we'll have a proper funeral. Boys, Gunn here is a friend of mine. Come on back inside and help us drink to Mort Wallen's memory!"

Hearty laughter broke out and men surged back inside the saloon in Gunn's and Jimbo's wake. Gunn felt himself being propelled from behind and only the long bar stopped him as men slapped him on the back, muttered greetings. Apparently, Gunn thought, any friend of Jimbo's was a friend of theirs.

He accepted the whiskey a bartender shoved in his fist, drank with the men lining the bar. Everyone wanted to know how he had managed to kill the two men that day and Gunn told them as simply as he could. He did not mention the warning he had received during the night. When they asked him about Wallen, he told them and the talk died down as men shrank into their own thoughts. Mort Wallen was one of them and he had died like the other men, strangled. This was a way of death that was frightening to men of their calibre. Some spoke up angrily, saying that only a coward would kill in such a way. Some brandished pistols until Jimbo calmed them down. The liquor poured freely and Gunn met so many men he could not remember their names. Soon, he began seeing them in a boozy haze as the whiskey kept coming.

Jimbo came up later, put an arm around Gunn's shoulder.

"They've brought Mort Wallen up from Roberts'," he said. "Some of the boys are fixing him up for a pine box."

"A funeral?"

"About sundown. His widder'll be there and his kids. It's going to be godawful. Why in hell you think we're all gettin' drunk. Hell, it could've been any of us out there, cold and stiff as an Alaskan mackerel."

"Any idea who the strangler is?"

"Not an inkling, friend."

"You think Torreon is behind the killings?"

"Torreon!" Jimbo spat. "Now there's a greaser fer ye! Claims all this land is his'n and Andy Worley knows better."

That was a new name to Gunn.

"Who's Worley?"

"One of the original settlers. Him and the Paxtons and Roberts laid claim to all the land along Luna Creek, got the deeds, put down hard cash. Smart man, but he says we can't take Torreon down without proof. Says it's muddy enough as it is without takin' the law into our own hands."

"What law?" asked Gunn, his tongue thickening.

"Exactly. There ain't no law out here. Folks trade in El

80

Paso and that's in Texas. It's so damned far to Santa Fe we might as well be in Mexico. But the boys respect Worley and have kept the peace."

"But the strangler. . . ."

"Chasin' shadows. He's slick, whoever he is. Slicker'n greased owl shit. We don't know if'n them night riders is Mex or white. No one's ever seen a face. Just a bunch of men with burlap sacks over their heads. Eye holes cut out."

"Lay for them," Gunn suggested.

"Hell!" Jimbo guffawed. "They got eyes ever'where. We tried that. Waited at one rancho and they hit another. Or, we spread out and they stay at home, laughin' at us."

Gunn saw the problem. Despite the number of drinks he'd put away, he saw the picture clear. Someone inside the settlers' group was tipping off the night riders. Or else they had some damned smart scouts.

"If Torreon is behind this, is he getting what he wants?" Gunn asked. "Any of the settlers packed up and left?"

"Nary a one," said Jimbo, proudly.

There was a murmur that threaded through the crowd and Gunn learned that a bunch was lining up outside in fifteen minutes or so. He pushed away the next drink, tried to clear his head. He asked what was going on, but no one paid him any attention.

"Fifteen minutes, end of the street," someone said.

Gunn struggled away from the bar. He was suffocating as men crowded up to the wood as if to get as many drinks in them as possible before having to leave. He wondered if the funeral was starting early. But no, they wouldn't have had time to prepare Wallen's coffin this soon.

Something else was up and everyone seemed to know about it except him. The outsider.

No one paid much attention to Gunn as he filed through the pack of men, found an uncrowded spot at the back where he could lean against the wall and catch his breath. He hadn't learned a hell of a lot, but more than he had expected. The banter was lighthearted, happy, but he sensed an undercurrent of anger. And something else. Fear. Most of the men in the room were afraid. Wallen's death had brought fear back into their lives. They remembered Paxton and Roberts and now they had another example of the strangler's work. The nightriders. Hiding under burlap sacks. Stealing their stock, killing only the men. And now they were drinking to forget how vulnerable they were. Drinking to forget their mortality. Drinking to screw up enough courage to fight back. Yet, they were fighting shadows. What they feared most, he guessed, was the unknown. Even putting a name to it didn't help . . . because the strangler, the nightriders, had no faces. They were nameless and so they loomed larger in their minds than someone they could see and touch and kill.

Someone touched Gunn's arm.

"I'm Patzy Summers," said a soft voice at his side.

Gunn looked down, saw a young woman with a low-cut bodice peering up at him with nut-brown eyes. Her blonde hair was startling, touched with peach, curled about her pear-shaped face. She smelled fresh, a contrast to the cigar and whiskey taint of the saloon.

"Gunn."

The woman broke into a smile. Half-moon creases at the corners of her mouth. A delicately painted mouth that curled back over even white teeth. A thin pert nose, slightly off-center. Flaring hips and probably trim ankles. She wore a dress that sported them, but it was full and she stood close.

"We have a mutual friend, it seems," she said. "A friend who has been asking about you."

"Oh?"

"Soo Li. Do you know her?"

Soo Li. He knew her. Had known her a long time. Had seen her only months ago in Taos. Before that, up in Montana. When she hadn't spoken English very well. A beautiful Chinese girl he had helped once, taken to bed.

"I thought she was in San Francisco."

"She was. She's here, in Palomas. Opening up a restaurant. She said you might come this way."

"How could she know that?"

"She didn't. Just a hunch."

"Good one. Where is she?"

"At the hotel, I think. Or at the Golden Bullock. That's her restaurant. Pretty fancy for these parts. Good food."

"I'd like to see her. Will you take me there?"

"I can't now. Aren't you going with the rest of them? Outside?"

"Where are they going?"

"Don't you know?" Patzy's eyes teased him, but he detected a trembling in her voice.

"No."

She turned away from him.

"Maybe you'd better go with them," she said.

As if on cue, voices arose in the saloon.

"Come on everybody!"

Gunn looked away from the woman and Jimbo was beckoning to him.

"Hey, Gunn," he called, "come on! You'll get a boot

out of this!"

Patzy Summers waved goodbye and Gunn found himself swept along with the crowd, the men jostling drunkenly, their breaths reeking with whiskey fumes. Outside, the sun hurt his eyes and his tooth throbbed with sudden pain.

The men strung out along the street, all heading in a pack toward the other end of town. Gunn asked no questions, but found himself alongside Jimbo, who had waited for him. They passed some new buildings and Gunn saw that the Golden Bullock was one of them. The name rang a bell. In one of the towns up north, possibly in one where he had first met Soo Li, the beautiful Chinese girl, there had been such a restaurant. Only it had been called The Golden Bull. Maybe she had named it such out of sentimental reasons. He was still puzzled as to why and how she had come to Palomas, but he shouldn't have been too surprised. When he had left her the first time, she had followed him, then gone on to San Francisco after he had promised to meet her there someday. Then, he had left her in Taos when he had met her again and she had been reluctant to part. She knew his restlessness and yet she had clung to him for a long time, begging him to return to San Francisco with her. Sensing that his feelings for her might grow into something permanent, he had declined. And now, Soo Li was here. Was she following him? And if so, how had she known he would come this way? Even he hadn't known that, for sure. He had told her he would probably come to California, by a southern route, and perhaps she had remembered. It made him uncomfortable. He didn't like being stalked by a woman. It was a threat to his freedom.

The crowd halted at the edge of town, formed a semi-circle.

Someone passed a bottle. Jimbo drank from it, handed it to Gunn.

"Drink this," he said. "You'll need it."

Gunn hesitated, winced from the pain in his tooth. The whiskey seemed to help dull the pain. He drank a healthy swallow, passed the bottle on to the man next to him.

Then he saw what they had come here for, and his stomach tightened.

Laughter rippled through the crowd. Uneasy laughter.

There, on a stack of wood and brush, stripped naked, were the bodies of the two men he had brought to Palomas.

Next to the pile of brush and lumber, a fire blazed.

Two men flanked the fire with unlit torches in their hands. These were sticks wrapped with oil-soaked bundles.

"What the hell is this?" Gunn asked Jimbo.

"Listen."

A man stepped out of the crowd, faced them.

"This is for Mort Wallen!" the man shouted. "This is for Palomas!"

An ugly cheer went up and the man came back into the crowd. The two men with torches dipped them into the fire and then lit the brush. The tinder-dry material caught. Flames rose in the pile, licked at the naked bodies of the two dead men.

Gunn turned away, suddenly sick.

The men threw their torches on the chests of the dead men as the flames rose higher. Soon, they were enveloped in a firestorm, and black smoke boiled out of the inferno, rose straight up into the air.

The sickly-sweet smell of burning flesh floated from the blaze. Men doubled over, vomited.

Gunn walked away, unwilling to look at this savagery. Jimbo watched him go, shrugged.

"What's the matter, stranger, no guts?" said a man in his path.

Gunn doubled up his fists.

"Shut up!" he said quietly, "and get the hell out of my way!"

CHAPTER NINE

Gunn woke with a yawn, stretched.

The sun was setting and he was glad he had checked into Luna House, taken a bath before lying down to sleep. Now, his body felt rested and the taste in his mouth was not as bad as it had been. Too much whiskey. It had taken longer to get the smell of burning human flesh out of his nostrils. He had done that by smoking two cigarettes in the tub downstairs and chewing a wad of Climax tobacco before lying down.

The slanting rays of the sun boiled the motes in the air until they sparkled like flecks of gold. The shade was half-pulled and he could see over the town, out to the land beyond Luna Creek. Part of it was in shadow, the rest was bathed in a pink glow.

His tooth was a mild thorn in his gums. A distant pain the only reminder that it was still there, still unhealed.

His stomach rumbled as he slid off the bed, naked except for shorts. He was hungry enough to eat jackrabbit.

The knock on the door startled him.

Who knew he was there?

No one.

He had walked to the hotel alone. It sat across from Jimbo's, but the streets had been practically deserted. A few people had gawked at the black smoke in the sky but had not spoken to him.

He picked up his pistol, walked barefoot to the door.

"Who is it?"

"Me?"

A woman's voice. At first Gunn didn't recognize it. Then, he realized that it was Patzy Summers.

"Patzy?"

"Yes. May I come in?"

"I'm not dressed."

"I've seen a man before. Please!"

Sheepishly, Gunn opened the door. He stood behind it, expecting to say a few words to her before she went away. Instead, Patzy swept into the room, her skirts rustling against her legs. He saw her ankles then, and they were slender. She smelled of perfume and she wore black.

Then he remembered.

The funeral!

It was supposed to start around dusk, and the sun was a boiling golden disc just above the far hills.

She looked at Gunn standing there, his pistol held in front of him, naked except for his new shorts, bought in El Paso the day before. They were wide-cut with an opening in the front. She stared at him, smiling.

"My," she said, "you are a fine figger of a man."

"I wasn't expecting company, Miss Summers."

"Patzy. I saw you check into the hotel. I thought you might want to go to the funeral with me and meet Soo Li afterwards. She's in El Paso, but should return tonight."

"I was planning on going. Fell asleep."

He kicked the door shut, walked back to the bed,

shoved his pistol back in its holster. While he was doing that, he heard the latch fall.

"There's some time before they start," she said. "The widow Wallen hasn't come in yet and just about every able-bodied man in town is dead drunk. But Mort's in a pine box and the grave is dug."

"I see. You going?"

"I thought you might escort me."

"I'd be proud to. But shouldn't you wait downstairs in the lobby? Might seem more proper. . . ."

"I came early on purpose, Gunn."

"I—I don't understand. . . ."

Patzy smiled becomingly. She hefted her purse, let it clump on the chair. She began untying the bonnet-string under her chin. She took off her bonnet, shook her hair free. She reached behind her and began fiddling at the back of her dress. Gunn looked at her in puzzled amazement.

"It's seldom we get an upstanding single man come through Palomas, Gunn. A lot of greasers, saddletramps, drifters. But I could tell when I first saw you you was a gentleman. At least you didn't stay with that pack when they burned those dead men. Oh, I know they were only doing what they thought was right, but it wasn't Christian, or decent."

"Hell, if it was my friend killed I might have done the same."

"Anyway," she said, slipping her dress from her shoulders, baring just the tops of her breasts coquettishly, "I hope you won't think bad of me for being so bold. Once Soo Li gets her hands on you I'll probably never see you again."

"Soo Li has no claim on me."

89

"No? She seems to think so. She went to a lot of trouble to find out where you might be."

"How could she know I was even down this far south?"

"Don't you know? Jed Randall. He wrote you about driving a herd up north. A herd of Luna Creek cattle."

Understanding flooded Gunn's mind. That explained how Soo Li had known where he would be. Sooner or later, he would probably have had to come to Palomas since he had agreed to help Jed on the cattle drive.

"Did Jed know about this?"

"I don't know. You'll have to ask him that. He'll be by one of these days. He's my brother."

"Your brother?"

"Yes. Didn't he tell you?"

"I knew he had a kid sister. But I thought she was. . . ."

"In Kansas. I know. I was married to a man named Delbert Summers. A thief, a gambler. He came down here two years ago and got himself killed. Left me without a penny. I've been working for Jimbo ever since. Oh, I'm not what you think. Jed wouldn't allow that. I do the cooking, clean up, some singing. It's been two years, Gunn, and in all that time I haven't seen a man I would give the time of day to. No, I take that back. It's been longer than two years. Delbert wasn't a man; he was, well, I won't shame his memory such as it is. But he never touched me after our wedding night. I was just someone he drug around to show off, to give himself the appearance of being manly."

Gunn saw that Patzy was about to cry. She bowed her head and started to pull her dress back up on her shoulders.

"I—I'm sorry," she said. "It all just came boiling up out of me. I—I couldn't help it. I saw you and I—I just went all fluttery inside. I'll get out. I won't bother you no more."

"No, please. Not like this."

His heart went out to her.

She sank down on the edge of the chair and he went to her. She began sobbing softly, holding her face in her hands.

He put his hands on her hair. It was soft, springy.

The sun hung on the edge of the hills, streamed the street outside with purples and pinks. Long shadows stretched away from the buildings, the hitchrails and roof supports. The light burned a ragged streak across the hills, clung to the earth like a distant forest fire.

Patzy looked up at him, at his shadowed face.

"Sometimes," she said, "I hurt so much I could cry. I do cry. Do you know what it's like? The loneliness? The sadness of being alone, wanting to be held, to be touched, to be loved? I can't stand it, but I do. I have. I saw you, Gunn, and something inside me melted. Tingled. It was like lightning striking. Like the shock I get sometimes at night when I comb my hair and it sparkles and crackles all over my body. When I was a girl I used to brush my hair in the dark and it would stand up, glow like fireflies. It was exciting and scary. That's the way I felt when you walked into Jimbo's today and I saw you standing taller than anyone else. I looked at your face and it was shining like that. I saw your scars and the dust on you and I could smell you across the room as if you were the only man there and I felt that tingle inside me, that scratch of lightning in my hair, on my arms. And I got all mushy inside and my knees got weak as if I was swimming in warm water with my clothes off, the water warm and cold at the same time. I hurt like that now and yet I feel ashamed and mad to talk to a man like this. Crazy mad as if I'm someone else listening to myself talk and say these things."

"You're not crazy."

He touched his fingers to her chin, held her face tilted up to him. In her eyes he saw the truth. He saw himself. His own yearnings. He saw the faint shadow of his wife, Laurie, and all the things she had said and done before she had died. He saw all of the women and himself, all the dark bedrooms, the shimmering light of lamps and candles and the white sheets, the pillows, the giving and the taking, the husky syllables of love words, the special wonder atop them, coupled with them as if those moments were the first moments on earth, of life itself, and the last somehow because the need was there and the joining was there and time was stopped like the stars were stopped sometimes like shining stones in a pool when the stream rushed by fast and sleek and never stopped but the stones glinted like stationary golden things that never moved and shined like eternity.

"Thank you," she whispered.

"Patzy," he said, "for what it's worth. I want you. Bad. This may not be the time . . . but. . . ."

"No," she said. "Don't say that. It's the best time of all. Instead of death, life. Instead of mourning, celebration. Please, Gunn. Now. Take me now."

Her passion radiated from her in invisible waves. As the room darkened, her fire burned even more brightly. He felt a stirring in his own loins. To refuse a woman in such circumstances would be cruel. Worse, an insult. She had offered herself honestly and simply from a complex mass of emotions. Yet he gave himself no credit. He knew how such things could happen. A small town, the feeling of isolation, fear of strangers, a lostness. All these things and more could bring a woman to offer herself so shamelessly to a man like himself, a drifter. Or, perhaps, there was only an uncertain chemistry at work. Something in him that she recognized, a kinship, an attraction of like people toward each other with no thought of the consequences.

And he did want her. He touched her bare shoulder and felt the warmth flood his loins.

He lifted her from the chair, slid her dress down. He kissed her neck, the hollow in her shoulder. She melted, sagged in his arms.

She rubbed a hand across the bulge in his crotch, grasped him desperately.

He stripped her clothes from her body, shed his own.

Naked, he drank her in. She came to him, gliding on bare feet, touched his ramrod-stiff organ, gasped.

"My knees are weak," she said.

He took her in his arms, felt the brush of bared breasts against his chest. Undressed, she was a child, willing, eager, yearning. He kissed her and she squeezed him until he felt the heat from her hand.

"You're big. Beautiful," she breathed.

The bed beckoned. He was dizzy with desire for her. Her body squirmed against his and he felt his lust ride up in him like a terrible hunger. There would be no more waiting. The sun was just a gold glint on the far horizon and the shadows in the room deepened with every pulsebeat, every throb of blood in his temple.

She was pliant, soft, willowy as he caressed her with gentle hands. There was a fear in her, beneath the boldness, a fear he could understand. She was afraid of being used, of being mistreated. And that was not his intention. He showed her with soothing strokes of his hand across her trembling belly mound, with the tender kisses he pelted on her face and mouth, her quivering neck. He found the hollows, the lobe of her ear. She shivered when he touched the pubic thatch between her legs, his finger tracing a path along the puffed lips of her sex.

Gradually, he felt the tautness drain from her tendons. Her flesh smoothed out, relaxed.

"Hurry," she said, "before the light goes. I want to see as much of you as I can."

He mounted her, thrusting himself between spread legs. Sank into her. Warmth flooded him. She was hot, wet, pneumatic inside.

She gasped at the suddenness of his entry, the unfamiliar intrusion.

Gunn sank deep.

Patzy bucked with a hard spasm.

"Yes, oh, yes, it's good."

It was good. She looked up at him, seeking reassurance in his pale eyes. But there were only the deep shadows, the contours of his face, as the room darkened. Her hands became her eyes. Roamed his shoulders and arms, slid over his back as he pumped her with slow smooth strokes. Gradually, she began to match his strokes, mashing her loins into his, blending with him in a shadowy ritual that excited her senses, honed her nerves to a keen edge of excitement.

Patzy spasmed again with a jolting rattle that caught her by surprise.

She cried out and clung to Gunn as if about to fall from

a great height. Hung on a cliff until the spasm passed and her senses realigned themselves.

"My God!" she gasped. "Nothing has ever been this good. Nothing."

"Just don't hold back," he said. "It'll always be good."

"It is as good for you as for me, Gunn?"

"Sure, Patzy."

"Yes. It has to be that way, doesn't it? Oh, don't stop. I'm going to give you as much as you're giving me."

True to her promise, Patzy unleashed the fury of her passion. All the pent-up, held-back, pressed-down instincts came rushing to the fore as she offered rhythmic loins against Gunn's driving thrusts. She drew him to her boiling depths and he scraped against her love-trigger with every stroke so that Patzy roiled the bedcovers with her thrashing.

Like some creature afraid of discovery, Patzy stifled her screams, the cries that swarmed from her throat spontaneously. Instead, she mewled and purred, emitted broken half-sounds of delight and wonder as if bereft of the knowledge of human speech, as if stricken dumb by the sheer ecstasy that gripped her body, her senses.

Gunn matched his strokes to her excitement, ebbing and flowing with her like a sea-tide. His ramming shaft swelled to white heat from the friction, the lava-hot broth in the depths of her sex. Most women, he knew, did not explode so, nor did they allow themselves to show the emotion generated by the act of sex itself. It was a shame and was as much a man's fault as a woman's and the way she was brought up. Yet he knew, from what Laurie had told him in secret, that there were ways a man could make a woman respond, could make her climax not once, but many times. Laurie had done that and most of the women since, but he knew, from listening to other men and women, that it was a rare thing, this passionate abandon.

And yet, it was the most natural thing in the world.

More natural than pretending that it was good when it wasn't, more natural than holding back out of propriety or a false code of morals. Gunn figured what a man and woman did in bed together was their business, not anyone else's, be it some staid queen across the ocean in England or the pinched-face schoolmarms who spoke to little girls of chastity and restraint.

With Laurie, Gunn had learned to hold back, not pop on the first plunge, good as it felt. By waiting, he gave more pleasure, received more in return. It was a simple thing, but overlooked by a lot of men who were quick as rabbits.

"How do you do it?" Patzy gasped, clinging to him after a series of rolling spasms that left her limp.

"Practice," Gunn said.

"Oh, you. . . ." She could see his teeth flash in the dark. She grinned back at him and he drew her hips up hard against him.

She cried out then, unable to keep her joy inside.

He let her sag back down and then raced her to the top of a lone high peak. Raced her and then waited until she thrashed. Exploded within her, splashed his seed deep as her fingernails dug into his shoulders.

"Mmmmmmmmmmmmmmmmmm!" she moaned.

And Gunn died the little death, collapsing on her warm sleek body.

Sated.

Full of her. Drained of life in a twinkling. After an awesome glimpse of what God must have felt at the moment of creation.

Voices drifted up from the street. Lazy, distorted. A dog yapped and a horse snorted.

Time sank lethargically into a drowsy pool and Gunn was suddenly hungry.

"Gunn?"

"Yeah?"

"Hold me. Kiss me. Before we go."

The kiss lasted a long time as lit torches splashed the room with ghostly light.

CHAPTER TEN

No one noticed as they blended into the funeral procession.

The crowd was solemn, following the torches up the street, the only sound the plod of horses, the creak of the wagon springs, the chant of a man reading words from the Good Book. Patzy did not look at Gunn, but kept her head bowed.

There was no church in Palomas. No preacher. The sky was a huge nave dotted with winking stars, the fingernail of moon.

At the cemetary, men carried the pine box to the edge of the rectangular hole in the earth.

"Ashes to ashes, dust to dust. . . ." intoned the voice and Gunn realized that it was Jimbo reading, his voice strangely ecclesiastical, hollow as a drum. He stood at the edge of the crowd, alone. Patzy had moved up to be near the widowed Sally Wallen and her stunned children. Gunn saw faces float atop dark torsos in the flickering light from the torches. He felt a knotting hatred strangle his stomach.

The box was lowered into the open grave and shovels clinked. Sally let out a mournful protest that was wordless, anguished. Gunn winced, turned away as the *swick-swick* of dirt began to fall on the pine lid of the coffin.

A face caught his eye.

He stopped, peered through a crack in the crowd.

Serena Paxton stood solemnly next to her mother, Winifred. Both women wore black. Serena's face was lit by a nearby torch, shimmered like a beauty mask. Winifred's head was bent, obscured by a veil. Gunn realized that she was staring into the hole where the casket had been lowered. Serena stared straight ahead, looking beyond the grave, into the dark night. She seemed a lovely statue frozen in space.

Then the crowd closed up and Serena's image disappeared from view.

Gunn started to walk away when a shadow detached itself from the group of men and women, approached him.

A man, angular, tall, dressed in a gray suit that smelled of dankness as if it had been hung in a cellar for years.

"Gunn?"

"Yes." Their voices were low.

"Talk to you?"

"Sure."

The man guided him by the elbow to a spot out of earshot of the onlookers.

"Andrew Worley," said the cadaverous man, extending a hand. "Serena told me some about you."

"I heard of you, too, Worley."

"Call me Andy."

"Andy. What's on your mind?"

"This has got to stop. Heard you come to help."

"If I can."

"Come out to Win Paxton's when this is over. Some of us'll be there. Like to hear your ideas."

Gunn tried to fathom the man's face, but the shadows were too deep. Worley's voice was low-pitched, but that might be only from whispering. He was faceless, without any recognizable character.

"Don't know as I have much to offer at this point. I'm listening, trying to figure out how good men can be killed so easy without anyone knowing who did it."

"We know who did it. You come. Listen. Maybe we can work together."

"I'll be there."

"Straight out the road that runs west along Luna Creek. A half hour's ride to the front gate. Another half hour to the house. You'll see the gate easy, north of the road. You ride at a canter, you'll have no trouble."

Gunn walked back to town alone, away from the crowd of grieving strangers.

He passed the Golden Bullock, saw that it was dark, like most of the other establishments in Palomas. Closed for the funeral, he thought. At any rate, Soo Li had probably not arrived from El Paso yet. He was curious about her, the coincidence of her being in Palomas not to be denied. Yet, their trails had crossed a time or two and he held a special place in his heart for her. He had not expected to see her until he went to San Francisco and he had had no firm plans for going there. The fact that she knew Patzy, who was Jed's sister, might account for her settling in Palomas, yet she would do far better in El Paso where there were more people. Yet, looking over the town, the country, Palomas could grow. There was water, good range, mild winters. People had settled in worse country. Against worse odds.

Torreon was the big question mark. What did he want with the land? It wasn't in Mexico, not even in Texas. Was that all there was to it? A simple, or complex, land squabble? It wasn't a question of water. The Luna didn't run down into Mexico and nobody had it blocked off anyway. Much of the land trouble he'd seen had been over water and boundaries. His own troubles up in Colorado with Coker had been because of a river changing course. Yet this did not seem to be the case here. Torreon wanted a huge chunk of land, claimed he had a right to it. Maybe he did. But the settlers seemed to have clear title, too. He'd have to find out where the survey stakes were and do some boundary cutting to make sure. The Paxtons ought to have the information he needed, or Worley. A man in his position, an outsider, had to make sure of the range and who was boss before he moved in and started throwing lead. So far, it seemed the land had too many owners, but it all boiled down to one clear-cut dispute: Torreon versus the American land-owners. Or was it that simple? That clear?

Gunn crossed the street, went into the hotel. The lobby was quiet, empty. Even the clerk was gone. His boots boomed on the board floor, echoed in the stillness. It was too damned quiet. Too empty. Somebody, he thought, had ought to mind the store. Or was the town so close-knit everybody went to a man's funeral?

He took out his key, upstairs, put it in the lock. It clattered. The lock turned on rusty fittings. Squeaked. The noise filled the hall.

The room was dark.

There was something different about it, though. A couple of things. His senses jangled.

The window was open.

101

There was no scent of Patzy's perfume anymore.

Instead, the taint of fresh smoke. From a cigar, or cigarette.

Gunn started to back out of the room when it came.

A sound like a hissing snake.

Something grabbed his wrist, jerked him forward.

He tumbled into the room, off-balance, pitching head first toward the floor.

The grip on his wrist was steel.

Pain shot through his forearm as hard fingers pressed to the bone.

He hit the floor with a hard thud.

Lights danced in his brain like the northern lights. Blackness crowded into the hollow of his skull where he had struck his head. He fought the dark with the panic of a drowning man.

A hard weight dropped on his back.

Gunn felt the breath go out of him. He twisted, wrenched his body away from the suffocating bulk on his back. He got his heels flat and pushed down as he rolled onto his back.

The weight dropped away.

Gunn's head cleared. He staggered to his feet.

The man grunted, came at him. A dark shadow in the room, moving fast.

Gunn braced himself for the rush. Still, he was surprised at the strength of the shorter man. He slid backward, felt the man's arms come up, hands reach for his neck.

He stared into black nothingness. It took him seconds to realize what it was. The man was faceless. Instead of a head, there was only a dark hood, twin eye holes cut in it. The feeling was eerie.

Strong hands grasped his neck. Squeezed.

Steel hands.

Gunn sucked in a breath, bulged his neck.

Thumbs dug into the soft flesh above his collar. Pain creased his consciousness. He hammered quick rights and lefts into the gut of his attacker. Felt the fists sink into hard flab. The grip on his neck tightened.

He would go down if he didn't break the death-grip.

The lights began to flash again.

At the edge of his brain, the black cloud formed, grew.

The man's arms were strong, his hands even stronger, it seemed.

Gunn brought a knee up hard. Into the groin of the strangler. A groan escaped from the cloth hood. The grip on his neck lessened. Gunn ducked, slid away, desperate now to escape those strangling hands.

The shadowy form of the man circled Gunn. The man was shorter, or hunched over enough so that he appeared shorter. Gunn circled, too, waiting in a half-crouch for the next rush. It came with a suddenness that surprised him.

Gunn felt a head jar into his gut, knocking the air out of his lungs.

At the same time, hands closed on his neck. Thumbs dug into his windpipe. His breath whistled as it was shut off and he sensed the blackness in his mind growing like a presence.

This time, he was ready.

He dropped to his back, kicked upward.

His assailant flew over Gunn's head, tumbling backwards.

Gunn turned, hurled himself at his attacker.

But the strangler moved too quickly. He was gone from

103

his position by the time Gunn landed on his chest. For a moment he couldn't see. Instead, he heard the labored sounds of breathing somewhere behind him. He twisted frantically, lunged toward the bed. His skull cracked against one of the posts. Lights sparked in his head.

A shape loomed over him.

There was no time to scoot away, no time to bring up a foot.

Instead, he braced himself for the hands, the crushing embrace of the killer in the room with him.

He brought his hands up defensively.

Gunn's grip tightened on powerful wrists. He felt his attacker's straining muscles as strong hands pushed in for the kill. Gunn squeezed hard, pushed the hands away from his throat.

Slowly, the hands gave way, but Gunn knew he couldn't keep up the pressure. The man was too strong, too determined. He would tire and the hands would come in again, fasten around his throat and shut off his wind. Then, it would be all over.

The attacker had the advantage. He was on his feet; Gunn was sitting down, pushing upward.

He could feel the man's breath hot on his face.

Stale breath, reeking of *mezcal,* onions.

Stifling.

Pain shot through Gunn's wrists. From the angle, they felt as if they would break if he exerted any more force.

The hands moved. The attacker twisted his wrists. Slick sweat drenched Gunn's palms. The hands slipped from his grip.

The hands came in from another direction.

In the dark, Gunn couldn't see.

He felt fingers scrape across his shoulders. Instinctively, he ducked. This act saved his life. His head came down, compressed his neck. Fingers tightened on his chin, but he had no neck for the assailant to squeeze.

"Back off, bastard!" Gunn husked.

The only answer was a grunt as the man tried to pull Gunn's chin up to get at his neck.

Gunn brought up a fist. His right hand slammed into the attacker's gut with a meaty thud.

The pressure on his chin relaxed.

Gunn slammed a left into the side of the man's head. There was not much force behind it. Enough, though, to enable him to roll away, get to his feet.

The strangler rushed Gunn.

Gunn sidestepped, back toward the open window.

Now, he was silhouetted.

The next rush came quickly.

Gunn stepped forward, then dropped to his knees.

He caught the charging man in the middle and heaved upward. He felt his muscles strain. There was a ripping sound and something came loose in Gunn's hand. His heart slammed against the walls of his chest, threatening to tear through the ribs and flesh. He let the man's own momentum help carry him upward and forward. Through the window. Glass shattered as the man crashed through.

There was a resounding thud and Gunn wheeled to see the dark shape hit the slope of a roof a few feet under the window. Quickly, the gray-eyed man drew his pistol. He hammered back, fired. Smoke, cloud-white, blossomed from the barrel. Black powder, acrid and biting, stung his nostrils. He heard the slash of wood splinters ripping loose as the ball gouged a path through wooden shingles.

Gunn leaned through the window, but the man was gone. Possibly, he had slid off the overhanging roof seconds before Gunn had fired. He had heard no sound of pain. Now, he heard no footsteps. He held a hard object in his hand. He put it in his pocket, unable to see what it was.

Holstering his pistol, Gunn raced from the room, out into the hall. He took the stairs a half dozen at a leap, streaked through the empty lobby into the street.

Behind the building, he saw the place where the man had landed. The dust was disturbed enough so that, when he struck a match, he could see it plain. There was no blood.

He looked around cautiously.

Waited.

Listened.

Nothing. No one.

Reluctantly, Gunn strode back into the hotel. On a hunch, he climbed over the counter.

The clerk was on the floor. Unconscious.

So that explained one thing.

But not who had attacked him. Or why.

As if anyone needed a reason in a town hanging on by the skin of its teeth. A town filling up with widows.

Gunn left the man where he was.

As he jumped down from the counter, Patzy Summers came through the door.

"What happened? I heard a shot!"

"I cracked one off."

"At who?"

"Someone up in my room. Who waited for me."

"But who. . . ."

"Yeah. Where have you been? At the funeral? See

106

anyone running down the street?"

Patzy shook her head.

"I was talking to Winifred and Serena. We were the last to leave."

Gunn's eyebrows went up.

"What about the widow?"

"Someone rode home with her. Serena and her mother were waiting for Worley to bring their wagon round."

"Oh? Worley left the funeral before they did?"

"Yes. I think. About the same time you did. I saw him talking to you and when I looked back around you both were gone."

"Interesting," said Gunn.

Patzy came up to him, looked at him rubbing his neck. She drew one of his hands away.

"You have an ugly bruise on your neck," she said.

"I'll live, I reckon."

"Gunn, do you think the strangler was in your room?"

"Well, somebody was up there. And he sure tried to pull the damper on my chimney."

"Oh no!"

"Look, Patzy. I don't have time to talk much now. I'm going out to Paxton's. Lock up my room, will you? Leave the key in the box. See if you can get help for that clerk lying back there. He's alive. Looks as if someone laid a pistol barrel side of his head."

Patzy gasped.

But Gunn was gone. She stared at the door, bit her lip.

Behind her, the clerk groaned.

CHAPTER ELEVEN

At the dark edge of Palomas, two shadows on horseback converged.

The horses stopped.

One man was breathing heavily.

The other, tall in the saddle, sat impatiently, his face shadowed by his hat brim, the night itself with its thin moon darkness.

"You get him?" asked the tall man who was not winded.

"No."

"He'll be trouble."

"He is trouble now."

"Yes. I should have known. I hoped. . . ."

"This one will not be easy, man."

"He must be killed." The tall man let out a sigh. "Dammit, you know that."

"It is not necessary to sweat. He can be killed. It is only the method that will be hard."

The tall man laughed harshly. A laugh that betrayed his nervousness and his fear. His unsureness.

"He has to die the same way as the others."

"Why? He is a big man. Very tall. As tall as yourself, *Señor*."

"If he does not die that way, the point will be missed. Torreon must know this. The pattern. That's what we're after. One man, two. Three. But this man. Gunn. He would be the key. The *llave*. Do you understand? If he dies this way, the rest will spook. It'll be all over."

"Don Diego," panted the shorter man, "does not have a patience without borders. Already he is restless."

"I know. I know. I am disappointed in you. You brag much. You had the man cornered. Why did he not die?"

The shorter man nudged his horse against the other's. He reached back into his saddlebag and withdrew a bottle. It gleamed faintly in the dim light. In the dark it was like an alien beacon. His swallowing was noisy.

"This is a man with a *sombra*, a shadow following him."

"Bullshit."

"It makes no difference to me what you believe. This is not an ordinary man. He gives me the shudders. There are such men."

"He's a fucking man. That's all."

"No, that is not all. He is very hard to kill. Maybe he cannot be killed until it is his time to die."

"I leave that up to you, pard. Get help if you have to, but I want his fucking breath choked off good."

The shorter man drew in a deep breath.

"I will try again. But I am going to talk to Don Diego first. He will understand what I am saying. This man has the *sombra*. That is his power. I think he will kill you someday, *Señor*."

"Torreon won't like it none."

"No, but he will decide what must be done."

"Him and me are partners, dammit. Kill this Gunn the

same way as the others and it's all over. The rest will pull out of here like a pack of jacks in a prairie fire."

"That is what you think. There is only one hitch."

"Yeah? What's that?"

"First, we must kill Gunn to start the fire."

****

Gunn didn't have any trouble finding the Paxton Ranch.

He saw the lights from far off long before he reached the front gate with its wooden legend arched over the road. PAXTON RANCH, the logs spelled out. He smelled cattle and wallow holes in the dark. Heard the cattle lowing off in the distance. Memories stirred in him, memories of a ranch up on the Cache de la Poudre in Colorado. Memories better left buried.

Someone in the yard challenged him. A torch was lit, flaring over a man's head.

"Who goes there?"

"Gunn."

"Yeah. Light down, go inside, pard."

Gunn touched his hat brim. Heard the hiss of the torch as it was dowsed in a watering trough. He hitched Duke up, next to several other horses. His boots rang on the porch. The door opened as he was about to knock.

Worley, slightly out of breath, stood there, holding the door.

"Just in time, Gunn. Come on in."

Gunn followed him through a small anteroom dripping with coats and hats, into the lighted living room. People stood and sat on the couches and chairs. Some held drinks in their hands.

"I'm glad you could come," said Winifred Paxton. "Andrew, find yourself a chair. Mr. Gunn, I believe Mr. Bobbitt has saved you a chair." Gunn saw Jimbo Bobbitt sitting by a window, an empty chair next to him. The big man smiled at him, pushed the chair forward to indicate where Gunn was to sit. Gunn stared at the chalk-white face of Serena Paxton as he made his way through the gauntlet of people. There were not that many, but they were spread apart in facing rows so that the group appeared larger than it was.

Serena looked at Gunn, then right past him as he sat down, his holster slapping against the chair leg. The small talk picked up, then died down as Winifred tapped her empty glass with her fingernails. The glass rang for silence.

"Gentlemen," she said, "I'm going to turn this over to Andrew. He knows my feelings. I know it's probably not the proper time to discuss this matter, after such a sad funeral, but . . . well, perhaps it is the proper time. Another one of our small number has been tragically murdered. We have a new widow in the Valley. It's got to be stopped."

Gunn marveled at her control. He would have thought she would have been on the verge of hysteria after this latest killing. The memory of her own husband's funeral must have been dredged up when they put Wallen in the ground. Yet Winifred was seemingly calm. She drifted back into the shadows. He heard a chair creak as the woman sat down.

Worley cleared his throat.

"They want us out of the Valley," he said. "That's plain. The womenfolks are plumb scared. And, I got to

111

admit, I'm scared myself some. Now, the way I figure it, we got to take action. Can't just sit around until all of us are choked to death."

"What you aim to do, Andy?" asked Jimbo.

"We got to put out some night riders. Maybe a couple of men at each rancho, ever' night, 'till we catch the hombres what are trying to drive us off'n our land."

"There aren't enough men to go around for a job like that," said one of the ranchers, a man named Millsap. "And who's going to ride at night when we're all so tuckered after a full day workin' cows?"

"Good point," said Worley, "but I don't see no way around it. Anybody else got any suggestions?"

Some of the men coughed. Serena looked at Gunn. He held her gaze until she turned away, a look of contempt in her eyes.

Gunn's tooth began to throb. He rammed the tip of his tongue against it. Felt it move. It was loose as hell. The pressure against his gums brought a fresh surge of pain to his jaw.

No one in the room said anything.

"I thought we might could raise money to hire a couple of men," continued Worley. "Riders who'd guard the ranches after the sun goes down. Men like you, Gunn."

Gunn froze.

Every eye in the room fastened on him. He squirmed uncomfortably in his chair. The silence rose around him like an invisible cloud.

"Mister Gunn has already been retained, I believe," said Serena, her voice frosty.

"He's an outsider," someone said.

"Yeah," agreed a man across the room from Gunn. "We don't know nothin' about him."

112

Voices rose in protest until Serena raised her hand.

"Enough! We're not getting anywhere this way. I have word that the titles to our lands are clear."

Winifred Paxton stepped forward, out of the shadows.

"I was just waiting to see what you all would do. We own the land. Not Torreon!"

A collective gasp issued from a dozen throats.

"I don't think it's going to do us a bit of good," she said, "but the papers arrived today. Confirmed. There is no question that the lands were clear and our titles all valid."

"But Torreon must know that," said Millsap.

"Yes, I'm sure he does. Mister Gunn, you haven't said anything. What do you think we ought to do?"

Gunn shifted his weight, rubbed his neck with a sweating hand.

"Seems to me you have a mighty determined feller trying to grab your lands. Going after this strangler in a bunch, or hiring outside help isn't going to help one bit. I told Miss Roberts I'd be around, look into things. I didn't hire out my gun, but I don't like what happened to Wallen. Or to Mister Paxton, even though I didn't know him. But now I got a personal stake in this."

"You better make that plain," said a man whose face was hidden from Gunn. "You don't own property here."

Gunn stood up.

"No," he said, "I don't. But after the funeral someone was in my room. A man, I reckon. He tried to squeeze my windpipe to a pulp."

Winifred's face turned chalk.

Serena drew in a breath, the air whistling through her teeth.

Worley's eyes narrowed.

Jimbo's mouth fell open like a trap door.

"Jesus," he whispered.

"Are you trying to tell us you were attacked—in your own room?" asked Winifred.

Gunn nodded, prodding his loose tooth with the tip of his tongue.

"And how did you manage to survive?" asked Serena, a mocking tone to her voice.

"Just lucky, I reckon."

Gunn returned her stare, a half-smile playing on his lips.

"I take it, then, you'll stay and help us?" asked Worley.

"I'm staying."

"Will you ride at night to protect the ranches in this valley?"

Gunn shook his head.

"I work alone. I don't take much to being put on regular rounds. Seems to me the strangler knows your business pretty well. He'll get on to that pretty quick likely."

Worley reacted as if slapped.

Serena stepped forward to avert any trouble. She put a hand on Worley's arm, spoke to the guests.

"There's food and drinks in the dining room. Help yourselves. I want to talk to Mister Gunn alone."

There were muttered grumblings but the promise of food and drink drew the crowd from the living room. Gunn sat in his chair, waiting, as Winifred followed the others. Serena stood in the center of the room, waiting too. She was as cool and calm as her name.

"Shall we step outside, Mister Gunn?"

"It's just Gunn. No mister."

114

"Very well."

Gunn followed her outside, pulled the door shut behind him, shutting off the light from the hallway.

Serena walked some distance from the house, her small boots scuffing in the hidden dust, creaking over the small stones underfoot.

A bullbat whiffled through the murky dark. A coyote yapped suddenly and then was still. Something scurried a few yards away, leaving the faint echo of clicking stones in its wake.

The silence grew up around them as Serena stopped near a low cactus bush, her form bathed in seeping light from a window at the far end of the house. She turned and Gunn halted a few feet away from her.

"I don't like your kind, Gunn," she said, her voice low, almost inaudible.

"My kind?"

"You're a drifter. You have no ties. You're here one minute, gone the next."

"We all have our faults, ma'am. And our prejudices."

"Your tongue is contemptible too, I see."

"You see a lot, I reckon. Or not very much."

Gunn didn't want to get into a verbal fight with the woman. She was a rare beauty, but he didn't hanker to her abuse. If she wanted to argue, he supposed it was best he keep his tongue still.

"I see enough."

"You call me out here to chew me out?"

"No. Of course not!" There was anger in her tone. Impatience. "I wanted to ask you what your real reason for being here was. You don't know Carrie. She doesn't know you. It was a chance meeting in town. Or was it? I'm very suspicious of you, Gunn. If that's your name."

115

"It's the name I use," he said quietly.

"Very well. I just hope you won't humiliate Carrie Roberts or cause any more grief around here."

"It's not my intention."

"I wanted to give you fair warning that I see through you, Gunn. Carrie may have fallen for your dubious charm, but I'm not that easy. You keep your distance and we might get along."

"Meaning?"

"Meaning I don't truck with saddle tramps like you. I've seen men like you come and go. You think you can walk up to any woman that takes your fancy and she'll fall right into your arms."

"You have that impression?"

"I—I do. I've seen the look in your eyes, Gunn. You think you can walk in here and take me to bed. I imagine you're quite experienced at that."

Gunn was silent.

He sensed that Serena was working through her own problems. If he had looked at her a certain way then it was because she wanted to be looked at in that way. He had not misjudged her. On the contrary, he figured Serena to be a lonely woman. More than lonely. Almost desperate. Yet she was gun-shy. Afraid. He wondered why.

"Don't you have anything to say?"

She moved closer to Gunn, as if challenging him.

"I reckon not. You've got my peg fitted into a hole and that's that."

"You bastard!" she husked.

Serena took another step, raised an arm as if to strike him.

Gunn lashed out, grabbed her upraised wrist. He drew

her close to his body. Her scent blossomed in his nostrils.

He pulled her roughly to him, reached up with his right hand and grasped her chin firmly, tilting her head slightly backwards.

"Let me loose!" she snapped.

Gunn looked at her full lips, squeezed her flesh gently.

He bent his head, kissed her hard.

Serena didn't respond.

Gunn slid his tongue out, laved her stiffened lips. Back and forth, touching her with his tongue tip, grazing her lips until his own tingled.

Her mouth opened slightly.

Gunn's tongue eased inside.

He released her wrist, slid an arm around her waist. Drew her close so that her breasts mashed against his chest.

Serena struggled.

But not very much.

Gunn found her tongue with his, laved it with saliva. Then, he broke the kiss.

Stared at her.

"Get out of here," she hissed. "Get out of here before I scream!"

Gunn smiled at her. Her eyes narrowed and sparkled with anger.

He touched a finger to the brim of his hat.

Walked toward his hitched horse.

A sound! The *click* of a hammer locking into the cocked position.

Gunn froze.

"No, Pablo," said Serena, "let him go. He didn't hurt me."

The Mexican stepped out of the shadows. The hackles

rose on the back of Gunn's neck.

He had been watched the whole time he was out there talking to Serena.

The bitch!

She had suckered him. Held all the aces. He was playing against a stacked deck.

He untwisted the reins, climbed into the saddle.

Serena stood there, gazing up at him defiantly as he rode close to her.

"See you again, ma'am," he said, saluting her. "You kiss right good."

Before she could reply, Gunn spurred Duke, stood in the stirrups as the horse rose up under him, hooves churning into a gallop.

CHAPTER TWELVE

The desk clerk looked up as Gunn strode to the counter for his key.

"Someone in your room to see you," he said.

Gunn's eyebrows went up a notch.

"Friend or foe?" he asked lightly.

The clerk was an elderly man with half-frame glasses perched on his bulbous nose. His eyes glittered like a ferret's and his hands shook.

"Says he's a friend. Woman with him. Chinee gal."

"This friend have a name?"

"Randall. Chinee gal's the one opening the hash house down the street."

Gunn smiled, gestured for his key.

"Key's upstairs."

"Thanks."

Gunn took his time going upstairs to his room. It was late and he was dog tired. He had expected Randall. Or even Soo Li. But not both of them at once. They must have been anxious to see him. To come here this late at night. He wondered how they had met. Either the world was getting smaller or else more people knew his business than he reckoned.

Jed stood up as Gunn entered the room.

He smiled as Gunn strode toward him.

On the bed, a shadow stirred. Soo Li sat there, smiling. "Jed."

"Gunn, old pard." The men shook hands. Jed Randall was a half a foot shorter than Gunn, with straw hair, wrinkles at the corners of his eyes. He was bow-legged from years in the saddle. His handshake was firm. He looked at Gunn with nut-brown eyes. Now he could see the resemblance between Jed and his sister, Patzy Summers.

"I see you know Soo Li."

"Hello, Gunn," said Soo Li, rising from the bed.

He turned away from Jed, took Soo Li in his arms. He held her tightly, felt her small breasts burn into his chest.

"Like old home week on the Osage," Gunn said, smiling.

He saw the bottle and glasses on the table. Jed sat down, began pouring three glasses full of whiskey.

"I knew you would be here," said Soo Li to Gunn. She was a sloe-eyed Chinese with jet-black hair, olive skin. Gunn noticed that her clothes were expensive. She wore the high collar open at the neck, the long slitted sheath dress that clung to her figure like paraffin on a duck's carcass. Under her long loose sleeves, he saw the flash of expensive jewelry. Her ear lobes were graced with a small pearl in each.

"I didn't know you knew Randall," he said, pulling out a chair for her. He took off his hat, sailed it toward the bed. Jed handed him his drink. There was an extra chair in the room. Gunn sat down, stretched out his long legs. The whiskey burned at the base of the bad tooth as he swirled it in his mouth. He winced.

"What's the matter, Gunn?" asked Jed. "Best whiskey in town."

"Got a game tooth."

"We had the clerk bring an extra chair," explained Soo Li. "Jed and I both wanted to talk to you tonight."

"Glad you did," said Gunn, swallowing the whiskey. The tooth pain dulled as the alcohol numbed the sore tissue around the root. "What's on your minds?"

"We heard about Wallen. Soo Li and I came in after the funeral was over. Heard talk in El Paso, too, about more trouble out this way." Randall leaned over the table, gripping his glass of whiskey. Soo Li sat straight in her chair, listening intently. "I met her a couple of months back when she was asking around about you. Helped her get men to build her restaurant here. I guess you met my sis, Patzy?"

Gunn nodded, glad to have some of the mystery cleared up.

"Go on," he said. "You didn't come all this way to chit-chat."

"Fact is, no. I got me a herd together. Want you to go in on the drive."

"The deal fell through I heard. People out here couldn't get one together. They've been rustled plumb short."

Randall nodded.

"This is another herd. Two thousand head. Man wants 'em drove to Abilene. Leave in two days."

"Who owns the herd?"

"Feller in El Paso what run into me. It's mostly white-faces. Two thousand beeves, Gunn."

"I'll look 'em over," said Gunn.

Jed grinned.

"Fair enough. Meet me for breakfast at Soo Li's. We'll ride into El Paso at dawn."

Jed stood up, slapped Gunn on the back.

"Good evenin', Soo Li," he said. "Gunn. . . ."

Gunn started to get up, but a look from Soo Li held him fast to his chair. The door slammed behind his friend. Gunn blinked at Soo Li. He saw, then, the mischievous twinkle in her eyes.

"You, uh, have a room here in the hotel?" he asked dumbly.

"No. I have a home. It was built fresh. Is that how you say it?"

Gunn laughed, nodded.

"Your English is improving. Wondered what happened to you after Taos."

"I returned to San Francisco with goods I bought for a cartel, made a great deal of money."

She sipped at her whiskey, peering at him over the rim of the glass. She looked, he thought, like some elfin creature. Her almond-shaped eyes danced with lamplight. She smelled of incense and perfume. He remembered Montana Territory and how she had followed him like a puppy when he had ridden out toward Utah. But he had sent her on to San Francisco, promising to meet her there. Instead, they had met in an unlikely town named Tres Piedras when he had the trouble with the gun thieves. They had made love again and parted again. Soo Li kept turning up, it seemed, not like a bad penny, but like a good luck omen. He smiled at her, cocked his head before he asked the next question.

"You want me to ride you home?"

"No. I want to stay here tonight. The house is empty, cold."

"Here? With me?"

"Yes. I have missed you, Gunn. I am much improved on my English talk and badly lacking in other experience."

"Other experience?"

"I have not known a man since you."

Soo Li blushed. Gunn knew that she was blushing by the way her eyelashes dipped and her face glowed with light. She was very becoming.

"We have had some good moments, you and I, Soo Li."

"Yes. I have missed you in my heart."

"It is not good to chase after a man."

"You are angry with me?"

He smiled, then laughed, to see her so petulant, uncertain.

"No. I care for you. But I am a loner, Soo Li. You know that."

"Not always."

"No, not always."

"Let me help you forget why you ride alone and run away from women."

"I don't run away from women."

Soo Li smiled, hers now the upper hand.

"Perhaps not. But when there is a forest fire, the lion runs as fast as the rabbit."

Gunn shook his head, watched her come to him. She put her arms around his waist, squeezed him tightly. He heard the silken rustle of her garment, smelled the woody scent of her dark hair. He put his arms around her, held her to him. She was petite, sinuous. Her warmth surged into his flesh.

"I will blow out the lamp if you wish," she said.

123

"No. I want to look at you, Soo Li. I have missed you, wondered about you."

"Thank you for telling me this."

She stepped away from him, began unfastening her dress, slipping the loops from the cloth buttons. He watched her for a moment, then pulled his shirt tails free, began unbuckling his gunbelt. Soo Li stepped out of her dress, slid her panties down bronzed legs. Her pert breasts jounced free of the constraining cloth of a black satin brassiere. The nipples jutted hard as pinto beans from the aureoles.

Naked, Gunn went to her, clasped her in his arms.

Melded his warmth with hers.

Soo Li buried her head in his arm, kissed the flesh of his muscle. Gunn felt a rippling tingle of pleasure that coursed from his elbow to his neck and down his spine. Soo Li peppered his arm and chest with kisses, nibbling at him like a small bird in a field of milo. Her tongue set off small fires, sent waves of heat to his loins. Amazed, surprised, Gunn stood there, a frozen statue, as the Chinese girl laved his flesh with her wet rough tongue.

Then, she dipped gracefully, sank to her knees.

She took his half-hard stalk in her hands, held the flesh reverently for a moment. Gunn stared down at her back, the skin taut, the spinal column pushing hard against the flat expanse of flesh. She looked up at him, then bent her head and began kissing the tip of his penis. Kissed it gently with only the faintest tongue-flick, until the organ stiffened with engorged blood.

Gunn grasped her hair as his knees went weak.

"You are beautiful, Gunn. So beautiful," she whispered.

Gunn gasped as she took him in her mouth.

124

Warm saliva drenched his manhood as Soo Li slid the length of his rock-hard cock deep into her throat. Her cheeks caved in as she applied suction, pulling on him gently but firmly. Her lips encased him, imparting a gentle pressure to his tautened skin.

She bathed him with warm saliva, licking his stalk like a cat lapping at a bone. Kneeling there, her body bathed in lampglow, she looked to be a nymph, something of spirit. Yet her touch was real. Gunn spread his legs to keep from sinking to the floor. The feeling in them had gone. The feeling was all in his loins.

Soo Li caressed his scrotum, fondling the sac with delicate fingers.

And still she kept suckling his swollen cock, drawing on it with a finesse that surprised Gunn. Her movement was slow, sure. Each stroke brought him closer to an explosion. Each flick of her tongue fanned the flames swarming in his loins until his fingers gripped her hair with a ferocity that was unintentional.

Just when he thought he could stand it no more, Soo Li stopped.

She gazed up at him, her lips wet.

He drew her up to him, her body sliding up his weakened legs.

Kissed her. Tasted the lemony salt of her saliva, the seepings of his manhood lingering in her mouth, on her lips.

"Do you want me to love you this way anymore?"

"No," he said gruffly. "I want you, Soo Li. All of you. You have learned much in San Francisco."

"What I have learned, I have learned from you."

"Well," he husked, "it was never sweeter."

Her breasts were warm sponges against his chest. The

nipples hard as buttons. He carried her to the bed, lay her down gently. She wriggled to the center, spread her legs to receive him. He looked at her a long moment, his temples throbbing with a blood desire that consumed him. She was beautiful as any woman he had ever seen. Lean and small, her legs were sleek as a thoroughbred's. Her ankles were small, sculptured to a fineness that he had forgotten since Taos. Her skin glowed tawny in the amber light of the lamp and she looked as sleek as a panther stalking prey.

She beckoned to him and Gunn lay beside her, began kissing the breast nearest him. Soo Li responded with a kittenish cry. Her body squirmed at the contact from his lips. Gunn took her breast in his mouth, teased the nipple with his tongue. Soo Li stroked his hair, gazed at him with a lambent light in her dark eyes. Gunn slid his mouth down her side, over to her tummy, his tongue working at her flesh like a lizard exploring a pile of rocks. He felt her wince slightly as he found her nest. His tongue flicked into the furrow, parted the crease. He tasted her honey, the sweet dew on the velvety inner lining of her sex.

"You would do that for me?" she breathed.

Gunn replied by probing deeper, his tongue-tip finding the small hard button that triggered Soo Li into a mild convulsion of pleasure.

Hot juices began to flow inside Soo Li's honeypot. Gunn lapped at her until her body shook with freshets of electricity. She spasmed, her legs flying up in the air, her loins quivering.

Then, he moved, slid atop her.

"Yes," she sighed. "Now!"

The tall man sank into her, the swollen lips of her sex parting the petals of a morning flower.

126

Soo Li bucked with another orgasm as his manhood slid across the point of her clitoris. Her hands grasped his broad shoulders, the fingers digging into his flesh.

Gunn sank deep until he was swathed in warm oils.

It took all of his resolve to keep from climaxing. He hung on, until the sweet pain of excitement passed. Soo Li spasmed even as he held himself still, deep inside her, even as he waited for his own lust to ebb.

The hot surge of blood subsided and his temples stopped throbbing. Soo Li fell back, exhausted, gazing up at him with tear-filled eyes.

"It is good," she said. "It is wonderful. Like before. Only it is much better than before."

"Yes," he said, and began plumbing her depths again as if he had just entered her for the first time. He stroked her slow and she undulated beneath him like a restless sea.

Again and again, she spasmed and bucked, but he held her in check, playing her senses as a master would play a flamenco guitar. Stroke, pause, plumb. Deep, shallow. Fast, slow. She rose and fell with him, falling into his sensual rhythms as easily as a dancer following an expert leader. Their lovemaking was a dance, now, a floating apart, a coming together that oozed sweat from their pores, sleeked their muscles until they glowed like tawny leopards feeding by firelight.

"Every touch of you. . . ."

"Hush, Soo Li. . . . I'm going to ride it on out. . . ."

"*Tochay, tochay,*" she murmured. "Thank you, Gunn. . . ."

Her eyes closed. He looked down at her, seeing her as if she was a sleeping princess from some far land across the sea, her bangs divided over her forehead, her eyelashes like overturned fences on her high cheekbones, or tiny yuccas uprooted by a quake of earth, delicate things like the stems of flowers, or the tongues of bees.

He plunged deep.

Lunged into her. Into Soo Li, who loved him, who took him like a wanton woman with a chaste look spread over her body like pure butter or honey. Lunged like a stallion into her deepest part, while his temples throbbed again and his loins swarmed with fire, his seed boiled in his scrotum like a pudding encased in a lidded pot.

He went deep; she went high.

Like arcing electricity.

Soo Li opened her eyes.

Gunn closed his.

Fire consumed him. Spread from his crotch to his brain like a track of burning powder. Creation itself closed in on him, buried him.

He exploded.

Burst out of the shell-egg of desire into that one terrible awesome moment when clouds blazed into silver fire and turned molten gold like sunset over Arizona Territory.

His seed splashed into her deepest pool as silent as rain tinkling on thick moss.

Soo Li clasped him, shrieked in Chinese, and thrashed like a woman speared on a spit.

Gunn held on to her frail golden body, a dying man with a heartbeat in his throat and brain. Held on to her and spilled himself while the clouds in his mind turned all colors, colors that seared and flashed and left no trace.

Hung on to her for dear life.

Dear life.

Felt the stallion in him die. Die the "little death." Die

the beautiful little death.

Soo Li. Sweet as honey.

Good as a gold Mexican peso.

She quivered for a long time. Her loins shook against his.

Soo Li drained him, her womanly muscles tugging on him long after his passion flew south like the band-tailed pigeon and the dove. Kept him inside her until he was emptied. A shell.

Until she spewed him out.

Until he was limp.

Sated.

Happy.

And she said the words again. In Chinese and in garbled English as she had so long ago.

As if they were children again.

As if one, or both of them, was about to die.

CHAPTER THIRTEEN

Don Diego Torreon snapped an unlit cigar in half.

The light in his eyes flared with a dangerous quirk, as if brush fires were breaking out on hillsides and lightning gripped the earth in a crazy design. He drummed four fingers on the table and punctuated the drumming with a hammering thumb. His left hand did this and his right hand ground the twin remnants of the cigar into crumbled leaves which dripped to the floor between his legs.

"Do not talk to me about shadows, about the *sombra*, you sonofabitch," he said. "Alejandro! Look at me!"

Alejandro Mendoza did not look at Don Diego.

Something was tightening in his gut so that he felt the blood draining from his face and a coldness in his head.

"It is not ordinary," mumbled Alejandro. "Rubio knows. He told me."

Torreon's face pulsed with hammered hatred. His dark skin flushed even darker; the cheekbones rouged as if warpaint had risen to the surface, drained out of his pores. His eyes flashed murderous.

The other men in the room shrank back into shadows, grasping their rifles, afraid to make sound. Sound of any kind.

They were all Mexicans. All of them respected Don Torreon. All of them were cold-blooded killers.

The back room of the *cantina* was large enough to hold two dozen men. There were half that number now. Their faces were gilded leather in the lamplight; their black pistols gleamed dully in the light. The wood on their pistol grips was worn smooth from use. Their boots were polished, their clothes faded, dusty. Some smoked small foul cigars, drank guardedly. Others chewed on tobacco or sipped at beer from rusty pails.

Torreon had called them in for one reason.

He was impatient. Impatient with *El Guante*. With the *gringo* bastard at Luna Creek.

A *mozo* from the *cantina* entered the back room.

"*Señor* Torreon? *Cual quiere usted? Mas licor? Mas cerveza?*"

"*Nada mas,*" said Torreon, withering the man with a look.

The *mozo* bowed toward his dirty apron and reentered the *cantina*.

One of the men by the door dipped his gaze when Torreon speared him with a look.

"Who let that man in?" asked a man named Dominguez. "You, Salcedo?"

"It makes no difference," said Torreon. "Kill the *mozo*. He saw my face."

Salcedo looked up, then, nodded. There was a chance to redeem himself.

"Now?"

"Now," said Torreon. "And don't let anyone else in but Rubio or Paddy."

"*Si, patron,*" said the other man at the door, who was

131

called Alonzo. Salcedo slipped out the door leading to the *cantina*.

Torreon smiled. He knew how Salcedo would do it. Quick and quiet. A long bladed knife slipped into the *mozo's* back. So quick and hard the *mozo* would not make a sound. It would happen outside and no one would know for sure he had done the deed. Even if anyone knew, no one would say anything. That was why Torreon had picked this *cantina* for the meeting. It was near the border, in a settlement that was run down, filthy, overrun with vermin. The men in the room with Torreon were the core of his cutthroat gang. The men who did his dirty work with no questions asked. He hated every one of them. None would ever greet him on the street in El Paso or Juarez. Not and live. None of them would ever be invited to his home. They were animals and he regretted the need for meeting them face to face now, but Paddy was busy in town and Amargo had not returned from his mission yet. Both men should have been there by now.

There was a knock at the back door.

Two taps, then two more. A pause, then a single tap. Torreon nodded.

Alejandro rose and opened the door.

Rubio Amargo stepped inside, blinked at the light from the lamps.

Torreon waved him over, poured *mezcal* in a glass. Rubio sat down, grasped the glass in a gloved hand, drank it straight. His eyes didn't water, nor did he make a sound. Torreon could almost hear the liquor hiss down Rubio's throat. He shuddered, looked into the eyes of the man who sat with him at the table.

"What good news do you bring me, Rubio?"

Rubio shook his head. The tension in the room seemed

to build from his chair, spread out until it gripped those standing around, watching.

"I am sorry to bring you bad news, *Patron*. I had Gunn in my hands; I could not kill him. The *gringo* escaped with not even a sore throat. I met with *El Flacco* later. He said that Gunn must die the same way as the others."

Torreon scowled. His hand dug out a cigar from his vest. He bit off the end, spat it to one side. One of the men struck a sulphur match, held it to the cigar end. Torreon sucked it to life, smacked his lips as he blew out a tendril of smoke.

"*El Flacco* is right. But the men are tired too, waiting for this to happen. Besides, there is other bad news. The claim has been decided in the settlers' favor."

"You expected that, *Patron*."

"Not so soon. Why did you not kill Gunn? He is different than the others?"

"Yes, Don Diego. He has the *sombra*."

"I see."

"You, I, no one, will kill this man easily."

"No. I am in accord with that." Torreon looked around at the other men. "We will wait for the Irishman. Then I will make my decision for what we must do."

Dominguez stepped forward. He wore bandaleros, two pistols low on his legs. He was an ugly man with a scar under his left eye.

"We should have action, *Patron*. We do not like to ride with *El Guante* in the dark and wait while he chokes the men to death like chickens. We want to shoot and ride. We want to burn these *gringo* settlers out of their homes."

Torreon knew that Dominguez was speaking for all the men. He was not angry for this outburst. When he had learned, earlier that day, that he had lost in the courts, he had already made up his mind that he would not allow the lands to slip from his grasp. He had other lands, but these were special. No one, not even Rubio knew the real reason he must have these lands. Paddy knew. It was his discovery, in fact. But no one else would know. There was already blood on the land. Before he was finished, there would be more.

"Calm yourself, Dominguez. We will listen to what Paddy has to say. Then, we will see."

Rubio poured himself another drink. Torreon looked at him closely. He had never seen Amargo rattled before, but he was rattled now. His hands did not shake, but there was a cast in his eyes that was unsettling. Somehow, this Gunn had become very important to the cause. He was a key. The fly in the salve. The cockroach in the soup. He had come from nowhere, but was already dealing himself into the game. If Paddy had concluded his business with Gunn's friend, Jed Randall, then maybe they could kill two birds with one stone.

Torreon looked at his pocket watch.

"The Irishman should have been here," said Rubio.

"Yes. He is late." Torreon got up from the table, paced the floor. His cigar burned down until it burned his fingers. He stamped it out on the dirt floor of the backroom. One of the men went into the *cantina* and brought back more beer and whiskey, another bottle of *mezcal*.

Salcedo came in a while later, grinning.

He drew a finger across his throat.

Torreon nodded, a look of contempt glimmering on his face.

The knock at the back door came. Everyone in the room jerked, then froze.

The taps were the same as Rubio Amargo had made an hour before.

The door was opened.

Paddy Ryan squinted, came up to Torreon, puffing for breath.

"You're late," said Torreon, who had sat back down, taken some whiskey.

"For good reason, me bucko," panted Ryan. "Oh, the sweetness of it, Don Diego, the pure sweetness of it. But, first, I'll have a chair and a taste of that fine whiskey settin' there. Lordie, I'm dry as a widow's cunt."

Torreon waited patiently as Paddy poured himself a healthy drink. The Irishman swigged the amber liquid down, his eyes bulging and dewing up. The cords in his neck stood out and his face flushed a bright rose.

Paddy wiped his mouth with his sleeve, caught his breath.

"Much news, Don Diego. Much news."

"I will hear it now," Torreon said sarcastically.

"Sure you will, Don Diego." Paddy leaned over the table conspiratorially. Rubio got out of his way, leaning back in his chair, flexing his gloved fingers as if tuning them up for more dirty work. "It's like this now. I saw Randall and he agreed to drive the herd out for us. Brands are changed. Papers bogused up so no one will know. And, my rich Mexican friend, he will use his *amigo* Gunn to make the drive."

"That is good news. When?"

"Tomorrow. But there's more."

"You tell me, Paddy. I'm listening."

"Sure. Randall hooked up with that Chink gal in Palomas. I follered them back to town. Was what took me so long. The Chink's shacked up with Gunn. Your idea to hold up the stuff she needs to open her hash house was a good 'un. The place is empty and she's gettin' the boots put to her by that lanky sonofabitch with the hard fists."

Torreon smiled. A light gleamed in his eye.

"You did well, my Irish friend," he said.

Paddy Ryan had proved out. He was a rough and tumble *Yanqui*, but he was educated, a geologist, who had come West with the Army, gotten in too many fights, been cashiered out, drifted with a wild bunch or two until he hooked up with Torreon. The wild streak in him had been tempered, but he was still a hard man to tangle with; fast on the draw, rough in a fair fight or foul. But Torreon wanted him for his brains, not his brawn. His discovery in the Luna Creek Valley had made Torreon realize that he had to regain land that had once belonged to his family. Now, it appeared he had lost, unless he could make the present circumstances work to his advantage. As he listened to Paddy, ideas were already forming in his mind. It was a matter of using his wits and the men around him to the best advantage.

"You could move right in there, I'm thinkin'," said Paddy. "With your man on the inside, a couple more men strangled ought to do it. I'd do it soon because one of these days someone else is going to stumble over those veins in the hills. Then you'll have armed riders keeping you out."

Torreon nodded, bit his lower lip.

He looked at the men around the room. They were all listening intently. He knew they couldn't be held back much longer. Still, he was not quite sure. Paddy was right, of course. The secret wouldn't be a secret much longer. And, his inside man, his partner, could make a mistake and be discovered before the ranchers were driven off the valuable land.

"It could be that this Gunn will be out of our hair for

136

awhile," said Torreon thoughtfully. His eye caught Amargo's. "You do not agree, Rubio?"

Rubio shook his head.

"You think that Gunn will drive the herd with Randall and by the time he returns, you will own the valley, eh, Don Diego?"

"It could happen that way. Gunn is only a thorn in the foot. The cattle drive will take him many days. By then, we will have driven out the ranchers and he will not find help to get us out."

"I do not think this will happen," said Rubio, his face darkening. He pulled out a knife, began digging at the thick dirt under a fingernail. "He will know there is something wrong with the herd."

"How?"

Rubio shrugged. "I do not know. But he will not go away. It is a feeling I have. Randall may not look too close at the brands, but this Gunn, he will."

Paddy took another drink of whiskey, looked at Rubio. He did not like the man, did not like the way he killed, but he respected him. Now, the hairs on the back of his neck were crawling.

"Paddy?" asked Torreon.

"Them brands are a first-rate job," he said. "He'd damn near have to skin a cow out to be sure."

"Then he will do that," said Rubio quietly.

Torreon considered the two men's opinions. He didn't like the way the wind was drifting his plans, moving them around, covering them up with the sands of doubt. He could almost feel the other men challenging him to defy Rubio's hunch about Gunn. The seeds of potential trouble were sown in the room. But he had known Rubio too long to doubt his "hunches." Rubio was a strange man, with few, if any friends. One reason for that was that he was something of a mystic. He believed in those things he could not see. He was part Yaqui and closer to that tribe than to his father's people.

Torreon stood up, his decision made.

"We will quarter in Lunita house," he said. "Until this Gunn is gone. If he does not leave, we will take over the Golden Bull in Palomas. I promise you that within three days we will be in Luna Creek Valley!"

Salcedo swore.

"We want to go now!" he shouted.

Some of the men agreed with him.

Torreon backed away as Salcedo, emboldened by the shouts of his fellows, stepped menacingly toward Torreon.

"Are you defying me, Salcedo?" Torreon asked.

"We are tired of waiting. *El Guante* is getting all the glory and he doesn't deserve anything. We are fighting men. We want the riches you promised us! I say we go now!"

Salcedo went into a fighting crouch. The rest of the men gasped, backed away.

"You would draw on me, Salcedo?" asked Torreon. "I, who brought you out of the filth of Juarez, put clothes on your back and gave you back your pride? You were a son of a whore and a whore's pimp. Now, you dare to raise your voice against me?"

"Draw your pistol, Don Diego. No more talk!"

Rubio half-stood, the knife in his hand.

Paddy cursed low, under his breath.

Torreon took a half-step backwards. His face flushed a leathery crimson.

Salcedo mistook the movement for a sign that Torreon was going to draw on him. His hand streaked toward the butt of his pistol.

138

'addy was faster.

A pistol appeared in his hand.

The hammer cocked with an audible click.

The pistol belched fire and lead.

Salcedo's .45 was half out of its holster when the slug from Paddy's gun ripped into his groin.

Torreon flinched.

Paddy fired again, taking dead aim on Salcedo's heart.

There was a boom. A flash of orange flame. The thunk of lead striking Salcedo's chest.

Bone splintered. Blood gushed.

Salcedo's eyes rolled into the back of his head. His mouth opened and closed as he tried vainly to suck in air.

He reeled backwards, his chest bubbling raw blood.

Paddy stepped forward, cocked his pistol again. He blew a hole just above the bridge of the Mexican's nose, hammering him into the floor. A man at the wall wretched. Vomit spewed from his mouth, onto his trousers, boots.

Another crossed himself.

"Anybody else?" asked Paddy, swinging his pistol.

There were no takers.

Still, Paddy held the smoking pistol in his hand. Cocked to fire.

"Don Diego," he said, "I think it's time we went somewhere's else to talk."

"We will go to the Barrio, to Lunita," said Torreon. "Leave that filth there for the flies to eat."

Paddy holstered his gun. Rubio slid his knife back in its sheath.

The silence in the *cantina* was deafening. No one came to investigate. Torreon was satisfied. The rebellion had been brief. Necessary.

Now the air was cleared.

CHAPTER FOURTEEN

Gunn woke up with a throbbing toothache.

It took him several seconds to clear his head. The room swam into focus. His mouth was stale, his tongue furry. Too much whiskey, the gum with the bad tooth was abscessed.

Beside him, Soo Li stirred.

Naked, she looked like a golden child.

"Soo Li," he whispered, holding on to the bed as if to quell the pain that shot through his jaw. "Time to get up."

The curtains were framed with a gray light. The sun was not yet up. It was out there, though, hanging behind the horizon, waiting for the earth to roll another foot.

Soo Li opened her eyes. Batted the lashes. Smiled.

Gunn kissed her on a nipple, nuzzling the nubbin in his mouth.

"I've got to meet Jed," he said. "Come daylight, I'll be heading for El Paso."

"I know," she said, sitting up, her breasts jouncing like melons on tethers. "I wish you didn't have to go."

"Might help Jed out on this. Reason I came down here in the first place. I don't think the ranchers here take much to my butting in."

"They ought to," she said.

She reached for him, picked up his limp organ. Squeezed it.

"It was beautiful last night, Gunn."

"You were beautiful."

"Did you think of Laurie? Was I your Laurie?"

"God damn you, Soo Li!"

"It doesn't make any difference. It was my own body. You made it sing like a thrush."

"Why do you ask such a thing?"

"Because I know," she said mysteriously.

Gunn clenched his lips.

She looked at him direct. He didn't avoid her gaze.

Soo Li knew.

She knew too damned much for her own good.

Yes, she had been Laurie. At first. She had to be. All the women had to be, at first. If not Laurie, then some part of Laurie.

He had never forgotten his murdered wife. He never would.

Laurie had died, yes. But her essence was everywhere. In this woman, in all the women.

And none of them, even Soo Li, could hold a candle to Laurie.

Gunn climbed out of bed.

Soo Li's hand slipped out of his lap.

"I'm sorry," she said. "I was too bold. I just wanted some of it to be me."

"Some of it was," he growled, pattering to the chair, pulling it up close to his pile of clothes. He dressed quickly, feeling Soo Li's eyes on him.

"Before you go, there is something I want to tell you,"

she said, when he was dressed.

Gunn fitted his hat to his head, adjusted it with a twist of hands to an angle that suited him.

"Talk fast," he smiled.

Soo Li frowned slightly, then tried to match Gunn's grin. But she was serious.

"I know you and Jed Randall were supposed to drive a herd of cows somewhere. I know that you just came to this place by accident. But I did not. And now I find troubles that puzzle me. My restaurant is almost finished. I am ready to open it. Yet there are some materials that have not arrived. I checked in El Paso and they give me, what do you say? the two talks."

"Double talk."

"Yes, that is it. When you go to El Paso, will you do me a favor? Ask at the Maxwell Freight Service where my packages are? These are certain fixtures I bought from back East and some linens, tableware. They should have been here some time ago."

"I'll check for you, Soo Li," said Gunn, touching the brim of his hat.

He thought that would end the conversation, but the Chinese woman came up to him, latched on to his arm as if to keep him from leaving.

"I know you have to go," she said softly, "but I want to know if I make you happy. I want to know, I think, if you will return. . . ."

Gunn twisted his head as if choked by a tight collar. Soo Li was putting pressure on him.

He looked down at her eyes. They were brown and moist, like nuts broken free of their moorings by a spring rain.

"Soo Li, don't make anything of this. Of anything. I'm

a drifter. A godamned widower who doesn't know one woman from another half the time. I like you. Like you a lot. Maybe there's times I could say, if I wasn't such a goldanged coward, that I loved you. But if I did, it would be a damned lie. Hell, look at me, cursing like a school kid. Truth is, you rattle me. You're something strange. A good woman, sure. A foreigner. I don't hold that against you none. Heck fire, I'm a foreigner myself most everywhere I go. Raised on Osage Creek in Arkansas, where we didn't have much schoolin' and all. You treated me fair, and I'm beholden to you. But I won't be strapped down by man or woman. I see the yearnin' in your eyes and I know damn sure what it is. If we was tucked away somewheres without the world crowdin' in, I'd hold you real tight and close and kill any man come near, but we both have our own trails to ride and you got to see that. I won't be a bad man to you, but I won't be your husband either. I wouldn't be a good enough one for a lady like yourself. Now, the more I talk, the more I'm going to get tanglefooted. So, let it be, Soo Li. We might see each other a time or two. If I think it's going to be permanent, I'll take a lock of your hair and keep it real close to me."

Tears rolled from Soo Li's eyes.

She squeezed his hand.

Then, she said something in Chinese.

Gunn nodded. He didn't know the words, but he knew what she meant. He leaned down, kissed her lightly on the lips.

And then he was gone.

****

Jed Randall squinted into the sun, loosened the

bandanna around his throat.

He leaned against the fence rail, watching Gunn walk through the milling herd of cattle. The cattle bawled and snorted as the tall man shoved them aside, looked at the brands.

The sun was up high and Jed knew they should have moved out already to make it to the first water hole by dark. There was a long dry stretch until Salt Basin and then another long drive to reach Red Bluff. From there on, things would get worse.

What the hell was Gunn looking for anyway? He had a tally sheet in his hand, another one with brand markings on it. The herd had been checked. A lot of brands, but all accounted for.

Flies boiled in the unusual November heat, rising up and falling as Gunn stalked through the herd, his head disappearing at times as he bent to check a vent brand, low on a cow's leg.

"Godamnit, Gunn, it's too late for that," called Jed. "Those cows are already road branded."

Gunn looked across a sea of brindle backs at Randall. Shook his head. Frowned.

Slowly, he made his way back to Randall, the cattle parting with shoves and kicks, closing in behind him. Gunn danced and sidestepped away from a swinging horn or an attempted butt, grinned from ear to ear.

When he came face to face with Jed, the smile disappeared.

"I don't like it," he said.

"What?" Randall's voice rose in a high-pitched whine. "What the hell?"

"You got a lot of vented brands in this herd."

"So? Cattle changed hands is all, Gunn. Man vents the

144

old hip brand, burns his own in right next to it. Commonest thing. I got the papers."

"You got some fancy iron work, too."

"Bullshit, Gunn. You don't want to help me drive these cows on down the road, you say so. But don't go pickin' nits on me now. We got to push like Billy-be-damned to make water by nightfall."

Gunn kicked a cow that had bulled in too close. Planted a bootheel on its rump. It flicked its tail, humped away.

"What do you want for that cow over there, Jed?" Gunn pointed to a brindle steer standing alone, looking at them wall-eyed. It had a hip brand next to a vented one, the road brand, JR, on its side and a jaw brand.

"Huh?"

"How much you figure to sell that steer for in Abilene?"

"Four dollars, maybe five."

Gunn's draw was so quick, Jed almost missed it.

One moment Gunn was standing straight, the next he was in a crouch. Leather hissed as he snatched his Colt free of the holster. The hammer cocking followed so close to the explosion he almost didn't hear it. White smoke billowed and the cattle bawled and tried to escape.

When the smoke cleared, the steer lay on its side, two legs twitching.

It was quiet as the cattle settled down. They had no place to go, so there was no stampede.

Before Jed could say anything, Gunn shoved his pistol back in its holster, drew his knife. He knelt down, slit the steer's throat. Blood gushed through the open wound.

"What the godamn. . . ." blurted Randall.

Gunn said nothing. But when the steer stopped

twitching and its eyes glazed over, Gunn made incisions in its four legs, began working the knife up the animal's belly. He skinned it carefully, sliding the knife between the hide and musculature with deft hand, careful eye. It took him a good half hour to lay the hide out, scrape the fat away from the underside. He stopped, after exposing the brands underneath and stood up. He wiped fat and the blade of his knife on his trouser leg, slid the wet knife back in its sheath.

Gunn handed Jed a five dollar bill fished from his pocket.

Then he built himself a smoke, lit it. The smoke swirled around his face and the flies beat the air with tiny transparent wings. The exposed carcass of the steer swarmed with black flies sucking at the fresh meat.

"You're plumb crazy, Gunn," said Randall.

"Yeah? Look at these brands now, friend."

Randall bent down, looked. He tilted his straw hat back on his head, turned pale.

"That Paxton's brand?" Gunn asked as he knelt down beside Randall. "A Lazy up left P."

"Was," said Randall. "Burned to a fucking Lazy 8."

"Like the rest of them. You got Double Diamond brands here, too. Like Wallen's straight up wide W. I'll bet my poke someone took a running iron and made two diamonds out of that one. I can buy another steer to make my point. . . ."

"That won't be needed, Gunn. Not now. I've sure as hell been suckered. Let me see that brand list."

Gunn handed him the paper which had been shoved into his belt.

Randall read it, frowned. Then read it again. Gunn watched him out of the corner of his eye. He did not know

146

much about Jed Randall, but he had worked with him in Wyoming, Colorado. Jed was a hard worker, but rootless. A drifter, like himself. He was inquisitive and seemed to have his ear to the ground for a lucrative deal. Perhaps that was why he had made a mistake this time. He had been too eager to take up the slack after the drive out of Luna Valley had failed to materialize. Still, he liked Randall. Trusted him. Until this moment, anyway. His own attitude depended on what Randall would do next. If he looked at the brands closely, as Gunn had, he would see that someone had been using him. Using them both.

Gunn tossed his cigarette into the dust, ground it out with his bootheel. His eyes scanned the pens. Men sat on rails a hundred yards away. He saw a bobbing sombrero through the rails to his left as a Mexican walked along the fence line. The hide now swarmed with flies, blotting out the altered brands.

"These fucking cattle are all rustled," said Randall grimly. His face had drained of color so that his skin had a chalky appearance. "All from the Luna Valley, I think. Jesus, Gunn."

"Yeah. Who are you making the drive for?"

"Feller named Jack Maxwell."

"Maxwell? He the one at the freight office?" Gunn thought of what Soo Li had told him earlier that morning. All kinds of gongs were clanging in his head.

"Max has several interests in El Paso. Owns the freight office, a land office, cattle brokerage, mining company. You name it."

"He's beginning to smell."

"Oh? You think he knows the cattle were rustled?"

"Let's find out. Roll up that hide."

"What about the outriders? They're here now. I hired

147

three Mex drovers."

Gunn saw the three men, their faces shaded under wide-brimmed sombreros. They sat on their horses beyond the corrals. One of them held the remuda together.

"Keep them on," Gunn said. "We're going to make the drive."

"Hey, wait a minute. . . ."

Gunn looked at Randall with narrowed eyes.

"Trust me," he said.

"Damned if I will, Gunn. I won't drive cattle with altered brands, cattle I know damned well are rustled."

"That's just what I wanted to hear, Jed," Gunn grinned. "And you'll damn sure drive these—but not to market. We're going to run them right back on the Luna Valley range."

Randall cursed again. Then he matched Gunn's grin. Gunn put a finger to his lips to indicate it was a secret between the two of them. Randall nodded, stooped over to roll up the fresh cow hide.

The drovers spoke to Randall in Spanish as the two men walked up to them.

"Tell them we'll be ready in thirty minutes," Gunn said, walking toward his own horse and Randall's. The animals were standing hip shot at a hitch rail a few yards from the corrals.

Gunn mounted up, waited for Jed.

Randall tied the rolled up hide to his saddle, swung up.

"Now what?" he asked.

"Let's go see this Maxwell."

"You won't like him none," said Randall.

"Well," said Gunn, "I don't expect I'll be too popular with him either."

****

Rubio Amargo's eyes glittered like agates.

He stood in the shadows of a small storage barn near the stockyards, watching the two *gringos* ride toward town. He had seen Randall stop and talk to the Mexican drovers who still waited, but now had dismounted, were lolling in the shade of their mounts.

Something was not right.

Why was Randall carrying a wet cowhide?

Rubio had only just arrived, expecting to see the herd move out. Instead, he saw only Gunn and Randall walking away from the pens, one of them carrying a fresh cowhide.

When they were gone, he stepped into the sunlight, whistled at the three drovers.

They looked his way.

"*Ven pa' 'ca,*" he called to one of the men. "*Andale', Hector!*"

Hector tossed a cigarette away, strode toward Rubio.

"*Andale',*" Rubio said again. Hector hurried.

"Where are those *gringos* going?" he asked. Hector shrugged.

"The cowhide?"

Hector told him what had happened. He had heard a shot, and the tall *gringo* had skinned out a steer. Randall had looked at some papers. He did not know what it was all about.

"Are they going to drive the cattle?"

"Yes, Rubio. Randall told us to wait. *Un media hora.*"

"A half hour?"

"They are going to Maxwell's," said Hector.

"Shit! Go back, Hector. Wait. If I whistle twice, two different notes, one high, one low, you shoot that tall *gringo* in the back. Fifty pesos in gold."

"Where are you going?"

"To see what they want with Maxwell."

"I think it is only to get some papers signed," said Hector, his eyes hooded by drooping cowls.

"It had better be. *Vete!* Remember, if I whistle just so, you kill the tall *gringo*. He is called Gunn."

"What about the other one? Randall?"

"I will see to it that he dies slow."

El Guante flexed his gloved fingers.

Hector shuddered and turned away.

Rubio gave the whistle. Hector spun.

"That's the way it will sound, *amigo*. Very innocent, no?"

Hector crossed himself, pulled his pistol as he turned and walked away.

He had no doubt that he would hear that whistle again.

And very soon.

CHAPTER FIFTEEN

Maxwell's office boasted three fronts on Bandera Street, not far from the stockyards.

One sign proclaimed: LAND OFFICE. Another: FREIGHT, HAULING. The third office building said: MAXWELL AND COMPANY, Mining, Geology, Stock Sales, Building Contracting.

Gunn and Randall dismounted, hitched their horses to a rail.

"Which one's Maxwell in?" Gunn asked.

"Freight office, most likely."

"Bring the hide," Gunn said, heading for the middle building.

A man looked up from a desk when the two men entered. He appeared to be a clerk, with papers strewn over his desk. Another desk was empty. There was a door leading to a back office or warehouse.

"Maxwell here?" asked Gunn.

"Who's asking?"

"I am, Barney," said Randall, stepping from behind Gunn. "Tell Max we'd like to see him."

Barney scowled.

"He's in his office. See if he'll talk to you, Randall."

Gunn took the rolled-up hide from Jed, glad that the fur side was out. The clerk went through the door. Gunn heard voices.

A large rawboned man came through the door a few moments later. His face was lined, beefy. He wore a battered felt hat, khakis, engineer's boots. His sleeves were rolled up. He wore an 1875 Remington .45 high on his hip, bullets jutting from the loops on the gunbelt. He had a pencil stuck behind one ear, a wad of chaw bulging one cheek.

"Yeah, Randall? Ain't you gone yet?" Jack Maxwell's voice was gravel laced with whiskey.

"Somethin's come up, Max," said Jed quietly.

"Hell, you got the papers, delivery date, destination. Don't see no hitches in that."

"There's a hitch," said Gunn.

He whipped the end of the hide, unfurled it like a flag, underside up.

"What the hell's this?" bellowed Maxwell.

"Check the brand," said Gunn. "Somebody took a running iron to the hip brand."

"Shit fire, that don't mean nothin'," growled Maxwell. "Vented brands is common as hen's teeth."

"This isn't a vented brand. It's altered. I could take this hide into a court of law anywhere in the country and get a rustler hung."

For the first time, Jack Maxwell gave Gunn a good look. He didn't like what he saw. He stopped sucking on the wad of tobacco in his mouth and met Gunn's gaze head on.

"Who in the fuck are you?" he challenged.

"The name's Gunn."

"So, what in hell you buttin' in here for. Randall

152

contracted to drive a herd of friggin' cows up to Abilene. Looks to me like you done kilt and skint one of them cows."

"I did," Gunn admitted.

"Why, you know that's. . . ."

"He paid for it," Randall said drily, enjoying Maxwell's discomfort. He pulled the five dollar bill from his pocket, plunked it on the counter. The door opened behind Maxwell and he half-turned to see who it was. It was Barney, the clerk.

"Somebody wants to see you, Mister Maxwell," he said.

"I'm busy."

"Important, he says."

Barney tried to get Maxwell's attention with frantic gestures, but the businessman had turned back to face Gunn and Randall.

"Tell 'em to wait. Five minutes." He looked at Gunn. "And that's about all the time you have, Mister, to state your business and clear out of my office. As you can see plain, I'm a busy man. Now, what is it you want? You kill one cow, skin it out and show me what you claim is an altered brand. I say your head's full of hay seeds. One cow out of a thousand head doesn't mean shit, Mister. You goin' to buy the whole friggin' herd to prove your point?"

"No," said Gunn quietly. "I'm just going to drive this one back where they belong."

"What?"

"You heard me. Come on, Jed, let's get to it."

Barney stood behind Maxwell, transfixed. Then he saw Maxwell's hand move toward his pistol. Quickly, he went back through the door.

"I wouldn't do that, Maxwell," Gunn said. "You can die awful fast with a fidgety hand like that."

Maxwell froze. His hand stopped in mid-move, hung there like an unwanted appendage.

"You bastard," he said under his breath.

Gunn smiled, turned on his heel and left, Randall behind him. He left the cowhide on the counter.

Maxwell watched them go, his face purpling with rage.

For a moment he considered drawing his pistol anyway and shooting Gunn in the back. But Randall gave him one last look and he knew he would be outgunned.

Instead, he turned, went into the back office, muttering dire threats.

Rubio Amargo was waiting for him.

"Well, Rubio," Maxwell barked, "you better tell Don Diego his fuckin' herd's goin' right back up to Luna Creek. Some sonofabitch name of Gunn just come in here and told me to go fuck myself. Barney, get that godamned cowhide off the counter and burn the sonofabitch!"

Barney shot from the office a good two inches off the ground. Maxwell looked mad enough to kill anybody who got in his way.

"You tell Don Diego," said Amargo. "He will not like it."

"No. Well, I had two men out there ready to gun me down."

"You are afraid of Gunn?"

"I'm not afraid of any man, Amargo. I'm just not stupid, that's all."

Rubio flexed his fingers. The gloves made an ominous stretching sound.

"It was a lot of work getting those cows," he said.

"Yeah, well, you can get 'em back again. He's takin'

'em over while you're standin' here jawin'."

"Maybe," said Amargo, frowning. He left through the back door of the office, through the freight warehouse.

Barney watched him go, his anger building.

"Godamned uppity fucking grease-ball," he said, then sat down in his chair.

It was only then that he began to shake all over.

****

Amargo rode hard back to the stockyards, taking a parallel course to the one Gunn and Randall were on. He beat them there by a good half a minute.

In the barn, he stood in shadow, watching the Mexican drovers.

When they stood up, facing in the direction of town, Amargo whistled. Two notes. One high, one low.

Hector heard the whistle, said something to his companions.

Rubio melted back into the shadows.

The long seconds ticked by.

****

Gunn thought about Maxwell, sized him up in his mind.

The man was not used to being faced down. He had almost gone for his pistol. Yet he had shown, in that instant of hesitation and decision, that he was not a dumb man. Many men, foiled that way, would have gone for it. Without regard to the consequences. Maxwell had not. Nor, to his credit, had he whined or called for help.

So, Maxwell was not out of it. Not yet.

Gunn kept looking over his shoulder.

Even so, with Maxwell it had been too easy.

There should have been someone following them. An alarm. Or something.

Something.

"What's the matter?" asked Randall. "You're mighty jumpy."

"Maxwell. He backed off, but his bristles were up."

"So? He backed off. That's the point."

"Maybe. I wouldn't fall asleep right now was I you, Jed."

"Huh?"

"Just mind you keep a sharp eye out."

"Just like Wyoming, huh? You get hunches like dogs get fleas."

"A hunch is like a gift from God, Jed. You don't get many of them and you don't get them all dressed out fancy. You just get them."

"Little voices?"

"Little or big, you better listen to them good."

Gunn flicked spurs into Duke's flanks, rode ahead. The two men and their horses rounded the corner, came onto the street leading straight to the stock pens.

He saw the three horses first.

They had been moved.

No sign of the three Mexican drovers.

The horses were tethered in a bunch. Packed together at the corral gate.

Gunn reined up. Randall caught up to him a moment later.

"Pull up," Gunn said quietly. His eyes were squinched slits, his jaw hard.

"Now what?" asked Randall, hauling up on his reins.

His horse sidled to a stop.

"The Mexicans. Where in hell are they?"

"Probably asleep somewhere."

"No."

Randall looked at Gunn impatiently. Gunn leaned over his saddle horn, his head behind Duke's neck and mane. He was looking straight at the remuda.

"What're you doing?" asked Randall.

"Counting legs."

Even as he said it, Gunn's right hand found his pistol butt, clamped around it.

"Get your pistol out, Jed. Too many legs in there. The three Mexicans are hiding in the remuda."

"I don't see a. . . ."

Just as Randall spoke, a Mexican stepped from the bunch of horses, cracked off a shot.

The bullet whined over Jed's head, sizzling the air.

Randall cursed, kicked his horse's flanks. Drew his pistol as his mount skittered into action.

Gunn was already moving, pistol in hand.

Duke raced straight for the exposed Mexican. Gunn leaned down over his horse's flanks, took aim.

Gunn's pistol bucked in his hand. Orange flame and white smoke erupted from the barrel. The Mexican tried to run back to the horses for protection, but the bullet caught him in the hip. He twisted crazily as one leg went out from under him. He went down thrashing.

It took Jed several seconds to bring his horse under control, rein him around so that he had a shot.

He saw Gunn riding straight for the massed pack of horses, hunched down so that he presented no target. The horses screamed in terror, tried to break free of the corral fence.

Another drover came out, low, sixgun blazing.

Gunn cut him down with a single shot, then swerved Duke away from the pack of horses.

Randall heard the air fry next to his ear.

Behind him, a pistol exploded.

Gunn's flank was exposed.

The two Mexicans lay sprawled on the ground.

The third one, Hector, was lying flat on his belly thirty yards away, taking aim on Gunn.

Randall swung his arm, trying to wheel his horse at the same time. He cracked off a shot. High and wide.

Gunn braked Duke, tried to swing him around.

Hector held his pistol with both hands. Took careful aim. Squeezed the trigger of his 1875 Model 3 Remington pistol. The pistol was shiny new. It belched fire and lead.

Duke staggered as the bullet tore into his flesh just behind his right foreleg, into the rib cage.

Gunn cursed, felt his boots jerked free of the stirrups. Duke went down. Gunn flew over the high side, hit the ground rolling. The horse blew bloody foam from his mouth, struggled to get up. Gunn felt the bile rise up in his throat.

The Mexican kept hammering away.

Bullets seared the air.

Gunn saw Randall ride on by, past the Mexican.

The sonofabitch was good. His bullets kept Gunn pinned down behind the mortally wounded Duke. He crawled toward the horse, peered over the saddle. He felt a tug at his scalp. His hat sailed away, ripped from his skull by a bullet.

Gunn crawled toward Duke's rump, head low.

Silence, as Hector reloaded.

Seeing his chance, Gunn raised his head over Duke's rump.

Behind him, he heard a *click*.

Wheeling, he saw one of the wounded Mexicans drawing a bead on him.

His scalp crawled with tiny spiders.

The black hole of the gun barrel seemed ominously close. The Mexican was no more than fifteen yards away, half-risen, his hand steady. Gunn whipped around fast, swung his Colt, hammering back. He fired, knowing his aim was off. At the same time, the wounded drover fired. Gunn heard the bullet thunk into Duke's neck.

Blood squirted onto the dirt.

Now, Gunn steadied. His eyes turned a cold gray as he hammered back, squeezed the trigger.

The Mexican's head exploded like a burst melon. Blood and brain matter flew in a half circle from the exit wound in the back of his head. His eyes glazed and he slumped over, dead.

"Look out, Gunn!" Randall yelled.

Gunn turned to see a shadow fall over his face.

Hector was there, leaping over Duke's twitching form, straight at Gunn.

There was no time to think about it.

Death was there. Its face a hideous bronze mask, a glint of hard dark eyes. It was the face of a savage.

Hector landed on both feet, legs spread wide for balance. The barrel of his pistol swung and held. On Gunn's face.

Gunn lay back, tipped his pistol, thumbing back the hammer, squeezing almost at the same time.

Then rolled toward the Mexican.

The explosion from Hector's pistol shattered Gunn's eardrums. Hot powder stung his face. Air burned his neck as the bullet plowed into the ground next to his head. Dirt spattered into his eyes, blinding him.

Something struck him hard, knocking the wind from his chest.

Hot sticky blood smeared his face.

Jed Randall rode up, leaped from the saddle.

"Gunn? Did he get you?"

Gunn pushed hard, shoving Hector's dead body from his own. There was a hole in the Mexican's throat. His eyes were closed. Death's face transfixed, frozen.

"Gunn?"

"I'm all right." Gunn stood up, brushed himself off. He ejected the empty hulls in his pistol, reloaded. Walked over to Duke. The horse was dead. Gunn's face hardened into a mask of hatred.

"Where'd you get these bastards?" he asked Randall.

"Over in Lunita, at a *cantina*. They were experienced drovers, would work for low pay. They had their own remuda."

"I'd like to kill them all again. For Duke over there. Help me get the saddle and bridle off and I'll catch up one of the Mexican mounts."

"You still going to drive these cattle back to Luna Creek?"

"I am."

"We'll need help."

"We'll do it ourselves. I'm running out of people to trust, Jed."

Jed saw the look. A chill shot up his spine. He coughed, lowered his head.

He didn't want Gunn to ever mistrust him.

160

"I'm sorry this happened, Gunn," he said. "I reckon I got to take the blame."

Gunn smiled. The smile was thin and humorless.

"Don't be too quick to judge yourself, Jed. There's others will do that soon enough."

Jed looked again at the dead men. Shuddered.

Gunn's judgment of them had been swift and relentless.

He was glad he wasn't one of them.

CHAPTER SIXTEEN

Rubio Amargo's hand trembled.

He knew now, for sure.

Gunn was followed by the *sombra*. By rights, he should be dead now. Braced by three good men. Hector was among the best there was. Fast, a dead shot. Now he, Elizando and Carlo, were dead. Dead as stones.

He rubbed the fingers of his right hand with his left. They had gone numb during the shootout.

For a long time he considered whether he might break out his rifle and try for a long shot. He watched the two men strip the dead horse of tack. Saw Gunn catch up one of Hector's horses, a sturdy black, saddle it. The opportunity was there.

But such a man would not go down that easy.

He was protected. By something. A shadow. A shadow that followed him, gave him that extra alertness that the hunted cougar had, that special sixth sense that few men possessed.

No, he would not try for Gunn this day.

His stomach boiled with the fluttering moths of fear. He had seen three men go down like chopped corn stalks.

It was one thing to kill at night, another to see death in

the daytime. Three men lying in the sunshine, their souls gone, their chests emptied of breath. It had all happened so fast. With not a wasted shot from Gunn. Truly, he was a man protected by angels.

This was not the way Rubio would choose to face a man.

Perhaps Gunn could be killed, after all.

His way.

At night, all the shadows were one shadow.

Perhaps then, Gunn's shadow would be lost among all the others.

****

Don Diego Torreon listened to Amargo's account of what happened at the stockyards with keen interest, his face darkening with each word Rubio spoke.

The others at the table listened too and their faces mirrored their disgust, their anger.

When Amargo was finished, one of them spoke up. He was spokesman for the others. His name was Miguel Oberon, and like the others, he was a man whose fuse was burning constantly. Yet he had not the character that Torreon possessed, nor was he a natural leader like Torreon. Instead, he was a political activist who had grown weary of living in poverty and seeing his ideals fail to take shape. He, like the others seated at the table in the Maguey's back room, was disillusioned with *La Causa*.

"It is all over, Don Diego," he said respectfully. "Your methods did not work. Instead of more money to finance our cause, we have ended up with a handful of sand. Instead of taking back our rightful lands by force, we have lost them through the *gringo* courts."

Torreon looked at the thin man who was speaking. He tried to hide the contempt he felt for Oberon and his ilk. Yes, he had been one of them once. An idealist, a chauvinist. But, unlike them, he had realized that nothing could be gained by following the law's course. Against their wishes, he had formulated his own plans. After discovering that the lands in question were much more than a symbol. There was gold and silver there, but of course, these men knew nothing of that. They were nationalists and gripers. Even if they had won, they would have bitched. They would have swaggered some and opened the lands to their people so that they could all gloat over their victory. And, afterwards, they would still be as poor as they were now.

"We are not finished yet, Miguel," Torreon said. "Let this Gunn drive the cattle back. Let the *gringos* think they have won. They will let down their guard and we will strike."

"No!" Oberon shouted, pounding his fist on the table top. "We have lost! We wanted to go in a body before the *gringo* courts and proclaim our cause, but you denied us this. We wanted to stand proud before them and insist on justice."

"*Baw!*" exclaimed Torreon. "You wanted to go before them and beg. Have you forgotten the words proclaimed by one of their own? I still have those words and you had better listen to them again."

"Frederick Douglass? One of their own?"

"A smart man. Listen!" Torreon took a folded piece of paper from his inside jacket pocket. He unfolded it and began reading. "'Those who profess to favor freedom, and yet deprecate agitation, are men who want crops without plowing up the ground.

" 'They want rain without thunder and lightning. They want the ocean without the awful roar of its waters.

" 'This struggle may be a moral one; or it may be a physical one; or it may be both moral and physical; but it must be a struggle.

" 'Power concedes nothing without a demand. It never did, and it never will.

" 'Find out just what people will submit to, and you have found out the exact amount of injustice and wrong which will be imposed upon them; and these will continue until they are resisted with either words or blows, or with both.' "

Oberon snorted as Torreon set the paper down.

"Words! You have found out that these people are rooted solid. This Gunn has given them the power to resist."

"Gunn will die," said Torreon. "I promise you that. You are giving up. Very well. I am not. I still believe in our cause."

"No, Don Diego, with all respect, you do not. You are a greedy man. We can see that. We listened to you and we were wrong. But we still have our pride. We will accept the decision of the *gringo* courts. They are wrong. You still have your interests there. We know that. You are a rich man. But you want more and you have a personal grudge at stake here. You have forgotten your origins and your people."

The men at the table nodded somberly, in full agreement with Oberon.

"You have forgotten the other words that Douglass said in that same context," said Oberon. "It might be well to remember them after hearing what Amargo has told you about Gunn."

165

"Fool!" said Torreon, losing his patience.

Oberon and the others stood up as one man. They were six and they looked at Torreon sadly, knowing they, and their cause, had been betrayed.

"Fool? Perhaps. But you'd better heed those words of that man Douglass. Remember, Don Diego? He also said: 'The limits of tyrants and prescribed by the endurance of those whom they oppress.'"

"Get out!" Torreon said coldly.

Oberon bowed in a mocking gesture of respect. The others shuffled out the back door.

Torreon waited until it was quiet, the room emptied of men he no longer felt compassion for, men who had deserted him because they were blind, stupid.

"Rubio, my friend," said Don Diego, "I do not want those men to return to their *jacales*. You know what to do. I will take care of this Gunn for you. I am leaving this afternoon, to see my daughter, Caridad. Take care of this matter for me and then report to me this night when it is safe."

"You will stay there?"

"Yes. It is time I plowed up some ground."

"Don Diego. . . ."

"Yes?"

"Nothing. I will do what you ask."

Rubio rose from his chair, put on his wide-brimmed sombrero.

Torreon pulled a cigar from his vest, struck a match. He watched it glow, but did not light the end of his cigar. Instead, he pulled the cigar from his mouth and snapped it in two. Then, he ground the tobacco into shreds, let the leaves fall through his fingers.

"Yes," he said quietly, "let us plow up some ground."

* * * * * * *

The burros made their way through a narrow defile, their hooves crunching on soft sand.

Miguel Oberon led the pack, his white shirt and trousers shining even whiter in the hot sun. Behind him, the others dressed in peon clothing once again, followed wearily.

The burro picked its way through cactus growing haphazardly in the arroyo.

Then, it stopped.

Brayed loudly.

Oberon looked up into the sun. The blaze scoured his eyes. He lifted a hand to shade them.

On to the top of the ravine he saw what appeared to be tall cactus. There were five of them.

Behind him, the others stopped too.

Too late, Miguel realized that the cactus plants were all moving. He saw something glint in the sunlight. Something shiny danced off his eye, like a mirror held in a child's hand.

Then, five orange flames spouted from the shiny objects. Explosions reverberated in the arroyo.

Miguel felt a fist slam into his chest. Then, a searing pain flooded him. He gasped for breath, felt himself flying from his burro. He fell onto the hot sand. His hand went to his chest, came away sticky with blood. It took him an eternity to realize it was his own blood. He could not breathe. He felt himself drowning.

More shots rang out.

But they were far away, like distant bugles.

They did not concern him.

Nothing concerned him anymore.

The sun turned cold and dimmed in the sky as if flying away from him at a high rate of speed.

****

It took the Sheriff less than an hour to sort out the facts of the shootout at the stockyards. He determined that the three Mexicans were all killed in self-defense.

The questioning drew a large crowd and Sheriff Dunlop refused to become involved in the matter of the cattle ownership. Several boys offered to help on the drive back to Luna Creek, so Gunn and Randall ended up with a dozen youngsters, all yelling and hollering, riding ponies and mules. The boys kept the herd in line as the mass of cattle moved out west from El Paso. More and more youngsters wanted to join the drive, but some dropped out, so the number of youthful drovers remained almost constant.

The drive did not take long. The last five miles found the herd strung out nearly half that distance, with wild boys riding up and down, chasing back the strays.

Dust hung in the air as the herd moved at a good clip through the dry country.

By early afternoon, when Gunn and Randall reached the edge of Palomas, a good sized crowd of ranchers and settlers had gathered out of curiosity.

Hank Worley rode out to meet Gunn, who pulled up to wait for him. Jed Randall rode back toward the end of the herd to be sure none of the cattle bolted as they entered the town itself.

"What's all this about?" asked Worley.

"I reckon you and the others have some cutting to do," said Gunn. "There's better'n a thousand head here, all with changed brands."

Worley looked over the herd.

"Recognize any of them?" Gunn asked.

"Maybe. Where'd you find 'em?"

Gunn told him, impatient with Worley's suspicions.

"Those double diamonds there are Wallen's," said Gunn. "Don't know if you have any cattle in this herd."

Worley shot Gunn a look and Gunn had his answer.

"I—I'm on the far end of the Valley. Didn't lose any," Worley explained.

Gunn was silent.

The cattle loped through the center of town as the people lining the street cheered them on.

An hour later, Gunn and Randall were sitting in Jimbo's Emporium, answering questions about the shootout, drinking warm beer. The bawling of the cattle had long since died away.

Patzy Summers waited on their table. Jimbo was expansive, buying drinks and getting half soused himself. It was a joyous occasion and many came up to Gunn and Randall, slapped them on the back.

"Looks like we got Torreon by the balls," exclaimed Jimbo.

"I wouldn't exactly put it that way," said Gunn. "Those Mexicans at the yards were just plumb unlucky. Sheriff said they were strangers in those parts."

"Well, no matter. You got the cattle back and gave folks a lot of hope."

Gunn was silent.

There were a lot of questions unanswered.

****

Serena Paxton saw the cloud of dust beyond Palomas. It was puzzling.

But not as puzzling as her visit to Carrie Roberts.

Carrie was gone.

So were all of her hands.

The house was deserted. The door open. Inside, she had found all the rooms empty. No note. No sign of violence.

The silence had been eerie.

She whipped the Arabian, touched rowelless spurs to its flanks. Something was going on and she meant to find out the meaning of the dust cloud.

Her hair blew in the wind as she rode hard for her ranch.

The milling cattle loomed up out of the dust. She heard the hoarse cries of men cutting cattle from the herd which was strung out over a good mile or so along Luna Creek.

Hank Worley rode out of the thick swirl of dust and cattle. His clothes were dusted with fine powder. His eyes peered at her from behind rims of grime.

"Serena. Appears you got your cattle back."

"How? Where did you find them?"

Quickly, he told her of Gunn's part in the drive.

"He says men were killed. Mexicans."

"How do you know the cattle are ours?"

"Oh, they belong to the Valley all right. Somebody got pretty fancy with a running iron. Yours are being cut out now."

Serena thought of Gunn and what he had done.

Perhaps she had misjudged him. Worley tipped his hat, rode back into the herd.

Slowly, she rode up to the house. Her men would tally

her stock and she'd get a report later. Right now, she had to collect her thoughts.

Winifred was waiting for her.

"I thought you were going to spend the day with Carrie," her mother said.

"She wasn't there. It's very peculiar, Mother. No one was there."

"That is strange. Come in, have some hot tea."

"Did you see what Hank brought us?"

"Yes, he told me all about it. I've sent one of the men into town."

"Why?"

"I want to personally thank that Gunn person for what he did."

"Mother!"

"Now, now, I won't hear another word about it. We owe the man thanks. I invited him to supper. So clean yourself up and make yourself pretty."

Serena looked at her mother sternly. Winifred's face was a mask. She wore an apron and her hair was tied back from her face. It was obvious she had already begun preparing a meal. That bothered Serena. Her mother never fussed in the kitchen. Not unless she wanted to impress someone, or cook an extraordinary meal for her father. And her father was gone, murdered.

Winifred shut the door, walked briskly toward the kitchen.

Serena shook her head, slipped off her hat.

Then, she looked at her mother's back.

Winifred was humming a song.

Something she had not done since losing her husband.

Nor had she, Serena realized, ever been in the kitchen since that night.

171

Was she, Serena wondered, inviting Gunn out for supper from gratitude or because she was attracted to him?

Gunn!

What was it about the man that made him so attractive when he was nothing but a saddle tramp, a drifter?

Was her mother inviting Gunn out because she was trying to be a matchmaker or had she fallen for his dubious charms?

Either way, she intended to see that Gunn had a thoroughly miserable evening.

The man wasn't her kind and she would have nothing whatsoever to do with him. Thank him, yes, and then keep her distance and see to it that Winifred kept hers.

Serena brushed off her hat and began loosening her blouse as she walked toward her bedroom.

From the kitchen, she could hear her mother singing the words of *Red River Valley*.

CHAPTER SEVENTEEN

Gunn looked at the man bearing the message.

A boy, really.

"You say that Mrs. Paxton wants me to come to supper?"

"Yep. Said it was right important."

Gunn shook his head, shrugged. "Winifred Paxton? Or Serena?"

"The Missus."

"Your name?"

"Todd Butterworth."

"Tell her I'll be there, Master Butterworth."

Gunn flipped the youth a silver dollar. The boy grinned.

"Thanks," he said. "I'll tell Mrs. Paxton."

Gunn closed the hotel room door, scratched the back of his head. He had been hoping that Soo Li would still be there, but she had gone. He would ride out to the Paxton place, but first he wanted to find the Chinese woman. Jed Randall was asleep and the two pints of beer he'd drunk weren't doing a whole hell of a lot for his own wakefulness.

He had forgotten to tell Maxwell to send Soo Li's

lumber on to Palomas. In the heat of his anger over the cattle, he had plumb forgot it. Now, he had to apologize to Soo Li. Make it up to her some way. That was the first item of business. He hoped she was at the Golden Bull. If not, he'd see her when he saw her. Maxwell probably wouldn't have sent the freight order out anyway. He had been pretty riled over the cattle.

It had been a long day. He wanted to soak in a hot tub for at least an hour. But he'd have to be content with splashing some cold water over his lean frame and towel off if he was to see Soo Li and ride out to the Paxton ranch. Quickly, he stripped out of his dusty clothes, filled the bowl with water from the pitcher. Someone had made the bed. Soo Li, maybe. It didn't matter. He probably wouldn't be sleeping in it this night. Patzy Summers had already given him an open invitation. No pressure, just left the welcome mat out for him.

He wished the invitation to supper had come from Serena. But maybe Serena had arranged it. That was probably the way things were done out there. Serena was over twenty-one, but she was still living in her mother's house. Her coolness might have softened some, now that she had gotten her cattle back. He hoped so. Serena was the finest woman he'd seen in many a moon. Her very aloofness added to her desireability. That was the nubbin. He didn't chase women. But Serena just begged for a man to throw a loop over her and haul her to the featherbed.

Gunn finished washing up and put on a clean shirt. He slapped his trousers as free of dust as he could get them and set his hat on his head. He glanced at his face in the mirror and knew it wouldn't win any prizes. It would have to do. If Serena couldn't take him as he was, then she was probably not as much woman as he'd figured.

****

Gunn knocked loudly on the front door of the Golden Bull.

A piece of paper flapped with the reverberations of his pounding. The strip of paper proclaimed: OPEN SOON.

The windows were dark. He tried to peer inside, through the gloom.

There were a few people on the street. They looked at him with idle curiosity. The sun was just about gone, a piece of it shimmering in the west like an arc of flame. The windows of the restaurant glistened with a patina of peach and russet.

Shadows flickered inside. Hovered. Were still.

Looking through the window, Gunn could almost hear the boards creak, the chandelier tick like a railroader's brass watch. He saw the covered tables, the shrouded chairs, the lamps and candles, all waiting to be brought to life, to be used by people.

A sound inside startled him.

He knocked on the door again.

"Soo Li?" he called. "Somebody in there?" He could almost hear his voice echo through the deserted restaurant. On a far wall, he saw a plaque, gilded, eerie in the darkening expanse of room. A bull's head, carved from wood in relief, its horns golden, its eyes opaque, like stones.

"Jesus," he muttered under his breath.

He walked away from the door, around to the side. The building was made of lapped siding. He could feel the coolness rising from the shaded earth. He touched the

175

wood, felt a slight warmth. He made his way to the back, saw a loading dock, steps leading up to another door.

He rapped sharply on the back door.

It opened, to his surprise.

Gunn stepped inside. The falling sun bounced off the open door, glinted off dancing motes of dust. He smelled new-cut wood. He walked through an empty storeroom not yet completed. There were tools lying about, dry shavings curled up from carpenter's iron planes.

"Soo Li!" he called softly.

A sound. The scraping of a shoe. Or boot.

Gunn tensed, forced himself to relax. His heart began pounding in his chest. The sound amplified, drummed in his ears. He stepped into the unfinished kitchen. Crates of utensils were stacked against a wall, piled on butcher block tables. He walked through the kitchen, opened a door.

"Soo Li!" he called again.

Silence.

Gunn took another step and heard a whispering sound.

He twisted, but something brushed against his face. He brought up his hands. Too late!

His fingers touched the rope briefly. Then, it tightened around his throat. He struggled. The rope tightened. He caught a glimpse of a dark shape. Small, masked. His hand touched silk as he slid down toward the floor, the edges of his brain turning black.

The rope dug into his neck. Shut off his air.

For a terrible moment in time he realized it was probably all over. He flexed his fingers, grabbed at the shirt of his attacker. His hand grasped a piece of smooth cloth. Silky smooth. He knew he would be finished if he didn't strike out, struggle. He let himself fall, then kicked hard with his right boot. He felt it crunch into soft flesh. He heard a cry, and the strangling rope relaxed enough to let him suck in air. He heard a ripping sound, felt a piece of cloth tear away in his hand.

He lashed out again with his foot. The toe of his boot thunked into a yielding belly. The rope fell away from his neck.

He was free!

Someone moved toward him as he tried to stand.

A blur. A shadow.

Gunn clawed for his pistol.

It was the wrong move.

He was looking at the head of his attacker, hoping to see who it was. The blow came from below as the strangler kicked him hard in the groin. Lights danced in his head. Pain shot up through his scrotum. Tears stung his eyes. He cried out in pain.

His hand grasped the butt of the Colt.

He forced himself to draw. But his vision blurred as the pain swelled.

Footsteps pattered on the floor. He heard a door slam. A crash. Then, another door closing hard.

He drew his pistol, staggered back into the kitchen.

Raced toward the storeroom.

Outside, the sun was down.

He looked both directions, listened.

Nothing.

A moment later, he heard hoofbeats. The horse was moving fast, but he could not see it. He turned, blindly, looking into the dimness of dusk. The hoofbeats faded from hearing.

Angrily, Gunn slammed the Colt back in its holster. That's when he realized he still had the piece of cloth in his left hand. He looked down at it, rubbed it between his fingers.

Soo Li?

Was she the strangler?

Whoever had attacked him had been small, wiry. Tough. Strong.

Gunn slipped the piece of silk into a pocket, strode around the building, back onto the main street.

The town was almost deserted at that hour.

Lamps glowed through some of the windows in the hotel, down at Jimbo's Emporium.

Gunn cursed, headed toward the stables. His tooth was throbbing again.

By the time he saddled up, his assailant would be long gone.

He felt his neck, remembered the rope. He went back to the restaurant, went inside. In the dark, he lit a match. The rope lay on the floor, like a dead snake. He picked it up. One more piece of evidence. Maybe. Useless by itself. Significant, perhaps.

In his hotel room, the other time, the strangler had not used a rope. Bare hands. That might mean something, might not. Still, he had some questions to ask. Maybe the answers would come.

****

"You set a mighty fine spread, Mrs. Paxton," Gunn said, patting his stomach in approval.

"Winifred, please. I'm glad you liked our humble fare."

There had been little talk during the meal. There was too much food to put away. Quail, a beef pot pie, fresh

178

hot tortillas, garbanzo beans in a small bowl, wine, potatoes, gravy, biscuits. Winifred and Serena both had thanked him for getting their cattle back when he had arrived, taken some bourbon with them before supper.

"There's dessert, Gunn," said Serena. "Hot apple pie with cheese."

"Yes, ma'am."

The serving maid, as if on cue, brought three plates with wedges of pie, slabbed with white homemade cheese. The maid returned, moments later, with coffee. And, still later, she brought brandy snifters and a full decanter on a tray. Winifred poured their glasses full.

"I'll have a sip of brandy with you and then ask you to excuse me. It's late for a woman of my age. I'm sure you two young people have some more talking to do."

Gunn looked at Serena. Her eyebrows went up imperceptibly, but she said nothing.

"I'll miss your company, ma'am," he said politely. "Thank you for having me to your table."

"The pleasure was all mine, Gunn."

Winifred rose from the table. Gunn stood up, but she waved him back down.

"Stay the night if you wish," she said. "The guest room is at your disposal."

Before Gunn could say anything, Winifred was gone.

A silence grew between him and Serena. She sipped her brandy slowly, looked at him. With wonder, he thought.

"Well, Gunn," she said, finally, "it's been an evening of surprises."

"Oh?"

"My mother never retires before midnight, for one thing. For another, she is very particular whom she asks

179

to stay over. There hasn't been a man sleeping in this house since my father died. Before that, only women guests occupied the guest room. And. . . ."

"And?"

"And, you surprise me."

"I don't see how."

"Your manners. You know which fork to use, which spoon."

"I've eaten food before."

"Don't get hostile. I thought you were a man of the trail, a common cowhand, but it's obvious you've known better days."

"None better than this one, with a few exceptions."

"Are you talking about the shooting this morning?"

"Yes. That, and what happened before I came here tonight. But I don't want to spoil your evening with unpleasantness."

"I assure you, Gunn, nothing you say could shock me. We've been through quite a bit here."

Gunn looked across the table at the poised and confident woman. She radiated a coolness that was enhanced by the lampglow. Yet he wondered if she was as strong as she pretended to be. In her eyes, he saw a distance that could mean she was vulnerable in certain matters. What was her breaking point? What made her so self-possessed? Was it all a facade, or was she really as distant as she appeared to be? The look in her eyes could well be a wariness borne of some tragic event in her past. Perhaps she was on her guard because of an ill-fated love affair.

"All right," said Gunn. "I went to the Golden Bull to see if Soo Li was there."

"Was she?"

"I don't know. Someone was there."

Serena's eyebrows raised slightly, but her eyes remained smokey, guarded.

"Who?"

"Maybe the strangler."

Serena gasped. Her composure seemed to crumble. But only for a moment. She regained her composure as Gunn went on.

"I wonder if you could tell me about your father, Wallen, the others. Was a rope used, or bare hands?"

Serena's eyes narrowed, turned to a cold hatred.

"You have a nerve bringing up such a subject. At my table, in my home!"

"I thought you could take it, Serena. Look, that was my neck being squeezed tonight. I should have gone down, but I didn't. My luck was good."

"Why do you think it might have been your Chinese girlfriend?"

"No, you answer my question first," he said, ignoring Serena's implication. "Rope or bare hands?"

Serena shuddered.

A mist appeared in her eyes, like dew. So, Gunn thought, she's not as cold as she puts on. She is human. Beneath that lovely coolness, there's a human being; tender, compassionate, warm, frightened.

She bowed her head, drew a corner of her napkin up to her eyes. She dabbed at the corners of them and, her composure regained once again, looked at Gunn with wide, frank eyes.

"Rope," she said. "The marks were burned into my— my father's neck. That's why I wondered who might have tried to kill you after the funeral. In your hotel room. You didn't mention a rope. At the time, I thought you

181

made it up."

"Why would I do that?"

"To draw attention away from yourself. If you were the guilty one."

"I see," said Gunn. Serena was running scared like everyone else in the Valley. "And Wallen?"

"Rope, too, I think. What are you getting at?"

"I think there may be two stranglers at work. Or, there could be someone who is imitating the strangler. Wanting to get rid of me, make it look like the work of the same man—or woman."

"Surely you don't think a woman is capable of choking a full-grown man to death. A woman would hardly be strong enough."

Gunn had considered that. He considered it again now. Serena had a point. It was one that had bothered him. He was almost sure that a man had tried to choke him senseless in his hotel room the other night. But, at the Golden Bull, he was equally convinced that his attacker had been a woman. Could it be a man and a woman working together? Husband and wife? Two lovers? But why? Father, daughter, perhaps. Or, could there be no connection? The more questions he asked himself, the more confusing the situation became.

"A woman, an ordinary woman, might be too weak or squeamish to choke a man to death," he said. "It is not easy to kill a man that way. But the rope is a tool. Let's say that our killer is a woman. How would she do it? Why would she do it?"

Serena blinked. Her face flushed slightly, then paled to alabaster. Gunn saw that he had given her quite a problem to mull over in her mind.

"I think," she said, "if it was me, I'd have to have a

very good reason to kill a man. Especially that way. And, I'd have to do it very fast."

Gunn smiled.

"Exactly! Only a person with a strong purpose would be able to stomach such a deed. Someone very cool and calm. Someone with a purpose, or a mission. Someone who could get close enough to the victim so the advantage was hers."

"You're saying that. . . ."

"Yes. Someone known to the victims, Serena. A friend."

CHAPTER EIGHTEEN

Serena's face went chalk-white.

For a moment, Gunn thought she was going to faint. He rose from the table, circled it, grasped her arms as she teetered in her chair.

"You all right?"

Serena gasped, shook her head.

"Air," she huffed. "I must have air."

Gunn lifted her to her feet as the maid came through the door, wearing a shocked expression on her face.

"Is the *señorita* ill?"

"I—I'll be all right, Elena. *Calmate,*" said Serena, allowing Gunn to support her weight as she stepped away from the table. "Just clean things up, please."

"*Si, señorita.*"

"You want to go outside, Serena?"

"Yes, please. I—I'm sorry. I just started thinking about my father and those other men. I could see them. Trusting someone, then. . . ."

"Don't think about it anymore. You can't help them."

Outside, the fresh air revived Serena. She was still shaky, but her breathing was better. In the darkness, Gunn couldn't see if the color had returned to her cheeks, but he was satisfied that she wasn't going to swoon. He wanted a cigarette, asked her permission to smoke.

"Yes. I like the smell of burning tobacco."

Another little surprise. A touch of humanness in a woman he thought had no feelings at all. It was her beauty that was extraordinary. Something in her face that reminded him of Laurie. Yet the two women were totally different. And, alike, as well. Laurie had been a calm person, hard to ruffle. Composed. Beautiful beyond comparison. An inner strength that had served her well during her last moments of life. He sensed that same core of strength in Serena. Yet Serena was hiding something. A fear that he could not detect, nor fathom.

Gunn built a cigarette, lit it. Serena leaned against a post on the porch, looked up at the night sky. Light from the living room lamp limned one side of her face, outlined her patrician profile. The smoke scratched at his lungs but his thinking began to lay down track, follow a straight course.

He thought of Hank Worley and the Irishman, of *El Guante* and Soo Li. The strangler could be any of those people. The question came down to a point of law he had heard about once. *Who stood to gain?* Worley might be working for Torreon, or against him. Maybe he had taken a page from Torreon's book and come up with his own scheme for taking over the Valley. But why? The creek lands were valuable, but not exclusive. Was he that hungry for land, for power? Torreon had to have a reason which could be political or strictly monetary. The Irishman worked for him. So did *El Guante*. But Soo Li? Why would she take up such a dangerous game? She had gone to considerable trouble and expense to build a restaurant. Was that only a front? It hardly seemed worth the effort. Yet she was mixed in this somehow, even if only as a victim. What about Serena and her mother? Were they completely in the clear? It would seem so. Unless they were completely heartless bitches who would murder old man Paxton to further their schemes. Well, in a world full of strange people, it was possible. Not likely, but possible. He had to consider Jack Maxwell, too. He was in there somewhere. Maybe only as a go-between, but he was in there. Right up to his Adam's apple.

The track petered out.

Then, Serena delivered him a shock that threw him right off what little track he had left.

"I went to see Carrie Roberts today," she said. "She wasn't there. No one was there. It was very odd."

"Yes? Why?"

"Because she was supposed to be there. And your friend, too."

"My friend?"

"The Chinese woman. Soo Li."

The bottom dropped out of Gunn's stomach. His knees turned to wobbly sticks and he had to brace himself against the porch rail. The cigarette dangled from his lips, forgotten.

"Why was Soo Li going there?" he asked, dreading the answer.

"Carrie wanted to see her. Something about the restaurant."

"Can't you pin it down any closer'n that?"

Serena shook her head.

"Soo Li and Carrie are friends. I gather that Carrie might have helped finance her venture."

Gunn picked his cigarette out of his mouth. It had gone suddenly tasteless. He thought back to the time he met Carrie Roberts. In El Paso. There was a ruckus on the street. Men bothering her driver. He had stepped in and that's how he had met Carrie. And Serena. Carrie had said she knew Jed Randall. Jed knew he had been coming to Sante Fe, had probably told Carrie a lot about him. Enough so that she knew him on sight.

"Jesus," Gunn said, starting to sweat.

"What?"

"Oh, nothing. I'm just wondering if I haven't been taken for six kinds of fool."

Serena came up to him, touched his hand. He smelled her fragrance. Her gesture surprised him. The touch was fleeting. He wondered if he had imagined it.

"I think you've been misjudged, Gunn. Not only by me, but by others."

"Serena, this is important. Carrie said her husband had been killed too. Do you know how it happened?"

"Not much. Her husband was seldom here. Wealthy, I assume."

"Strangled?"

"Yes."

"Rope?"

"Why—I've forgotten. But now that you mention it, I don't think so. He was the first one, buried at a private ceremony. None of us saw him or heard much about his death. We all just assumed. . . ."

"Dammit, that's what I've been doing!" Gunn exclaimed, driving a fist into the porch railing. "I've been taking every thing at face value and not biting into the damned dollar. Serena, I think I've been part of all this without meaning to. I mean I think someone wanted me to come out here and get mixed up with you people only so that the real killer would not be suspicioned!"

"I—I don't follow you, Gunn."

"I'm not sure I can lay it all out plain just yet. But maybe I'm just some raw bait dragged across a trail. A diversion. It could be that Torreon himself wasn't in on this part of it. Fact is, I'll bet that he wasn't."

"Don't blame yourself." Her tone of voice changed then. A note of sympathy and something more shaded her words. Again, she touched his hand on the porch rail. This time, it lingered. He didn't want it ever to go away. A surge of feeling rose up in him. To have her so near, to have her touching him.

"I still don't know what I'm supposed to know," he said quietly. "There's something just out there, but I can't lay hold of it. It's been there all the time, but I didn't see it. Something I ought to have seen, but didn't. Someone who's behind these murders but works alone. Yet there's a connection to Torreon. And, more than one, I'm thinking."

"I've thought about it, too, Gunn. Ever since my father died. I think that's when I started to hate. And that's not good. I've seen you struggling with your own conscience. You're not an actor. You're real. Everything you've said tonight has made me realize what a fool I've been myself."

"No, Serena. . . ."

"Hush. Let me finish. A long time ago, I loved a man. I thought he was good. He was handsome, strong, promising. He was the son of a wealthy family in Georgia. Cotton. He courted me, wanted me to marry him. In fact, he wanted me to run away with him. He needed money, so I gave it to him. I ran away with him. I let him make love to me the night we arrived in Fort Worth since I assumed he would marry me in a few days. He took my money, left me stranded, ashamed, humiliated. I tried to find him, since I still believed that it was all a mistake. I was without funds, but I started looking for Wade. To my regret, I found him. He was in a gambling hall with another woman. Drunk, almost broke. He—he said he hated me and I left, sold my clothes and took the stage back home. I've never left again. But I hear about Wade every now and then. His family disowned him. He's a poor cowboy with a terrible disease he got in Houston. He. . . ."

"He is only one man. One experience. You can't judge all men by him, Serena."

"I—I realize that now."

"Do you?"

"What do you mean?"

"You're letting the man ruin your own life. He's already ruined his. As long as you keep that particular memory, you'll suffer."

"You're right, Gunn, I'm so scared." She clung to him, then. A desperate woman, too long neglected. He felt her body press against his and knew he couldn't stand it any longer. He wanted her. Yet, she had to make the first move. He was no solution to her problems. He knew that. But he was attracted to her. Strongly attracted.

"There's nothing I can offer you," he said honestly.

"You've already given me a great deal. Your understanding. Maybe your sympathy."

"You don't want sympathy."

"No, Gunn. Not that."

"Love? Even if it's only for a short while?"

"Yes!" she husked. She rubbed her loins against his.

189

He felt her heat seep through his trousers, warm his crotch. She put her arms around his neck, drew his mouth down to hers. She offered her lips.

He kissed her hard.

Their lips met hungrily and he knew it would happen. Her mouth opened like a wet flower. Her tongue slithered into his mouth. A stab of pain shot through his gums as she touched the tender tooth. He winced and she clutched him even harder.

When they broke, Serena was panting.

Her hands trembled.

"Gunn, take me before I . . . before I run away from you. . . ."

"Serena, I won't deny it. I want you. But only if. . . ."

"No 'if.' I want you too. Desperately. Only, hurry, before I get too scared to take you to my bed."

He looked at her. Saw the desire in her eyes.

She wanted him.

Serena was ready.

****

The house was quiet. Creaking with a tick-tick as the wood stretched and contracted.

Serena's bedroom, lavishly feminine, was bathed in a warm light from the pewter lamp on her dressing table. The light was magnified by the mirror, flowed over the bearskin rug in the center of the room.

Naked, Gunn went to her, his body shielding her from the lampglow.

Her eyes glistened like diamonds in a pool.

They shone with a startling lust.

Serena gazed at Gunn's manhood, licked her lips.

"I'm not surprised," she breathed. "I knew you would be magnificent."

He slid beside her, took her in his arms.

Her flesh was warm, pliant. She wriggled against him. Her breasts flattened against his chest as he squeezed her hard. Her tallness made them fit together like a pair of spoons. His rock-hard cock found her nest, nuzzled up against it.

Serena shivered at the sudden contact.

Gunn kissed her breasts. Nibbled at her nipples, felt them grow and stiffen under the deft manipulation of his probing tongue.

"Oh, stop, Gunn, stop," Serena begged.

Gunn stopped. Looked at her sleek body. A sculpture, bronzed by the light. The breasts, perfect, the nipples hard nubbins, the tummy flat. Long sweet legs, trim ankles.

"Don't stop," she said.

"But you said. . . ."

"I lied, Gunn."

She spread her legs, beckoned for him to mount her.

He climbed aboard, felt her take his throbbing stalk in her hand. She clasped his swollen cock with delicate fingers, pulled him down to her steaming thatch. Her musk rose up, taunted his nostrils. The scent of her was like a damp forest warmed by morning sun, like the fresh-tilled earth of Arkansas when the seed is going in during a rain shower.

Gunn dipped to her. Sank past her primed portals. Sank into the steaming cauldron of her sex.

Felt her fingers dig into his arm muscles like shrouded talons. No pain, just the urgency of desire transmitted through flesh.

191

And her body rose up to meet his. Her hips crashed into his thighs. He shot deeper still and she twitched from head to toe with a convulsive snap as if a whip had been laid across her buttocks.

"Oh!" she wailed. "Stop, oh, please stop!"

"You don't mean it," he husked.

"No. No, don't stop. Not now. I—I'm. . . ."

And she was. Coming like a fountain. Like a spring freshet burst from the rock-vault of a mountain wall. Bubbling inside like the ponds on the Yellowstone. The dank heat sucked at him, drew him down through the folds of flesh into a blinding world of the senses where every touch was magic, every soft word a shout, every moment a brilliant eternity.

"Yes," she gasped. "Oh, Gunn, I'm not sorry, not sorry at all. I'm glad you came here, glad you took me like this. I've wanted something like this for so long. I want you to keep on, don't stop, don't listen to me. I'm crazy with you. Crazy for your hardness, for that hard thing inside me."

She babbled, but he no longer heard her.

It was all he could do to hold himself back, keep from bursting inside her. She was more than he expected, more than any man could expect from a woman. All silk and teeth, all liquid movement, flashes of stars and halos of rainbows, exploding fireworks, swift lava streams, green far meadows leaping with summer and the sweet warm sunshine.

He slammed into her. And she yielded. There was no pain in his thrusts. Just an energy that thrilled him, shot through her flesh like the sparks off a flywheel.

He stopped and she screamed for him.

Clawed for him.

Gunn caught his breath and smiled.

Serena smiled back at him.

And then he didn't stop, but plowed on, plumbing her smoking pudding until she threw her legs up in the air and spasmed like some quivering animal.

He let it all go. Shot his seed into her as she shook and sobbed. Felt it boil into her womb like a squirting artery, like his own dark blood.

It was as sweet a moment as any in his life.

Fleeting as a spring morning.

He fell onto her, exhausted, as the wick burned low in the lamp and the room darkened.

She spewed him out, his limpness complete.

A cold dead serpent on her dank nest.

Serena shuddered one last time.

CHAPTER NINETEEN

Morning was a chill November gruel.

The sky hung low, pale clouds burying the last of the sun as they rolled toward the eastern horizon.

Gunn shook the sleep off with a twist of his head, spurred the horse into a slow gallop.

It was hard to leave Serena.

After last night.

The dawn time together had been just as sweet. Tough to leave her. Tough to leave a woman so full of loving. A woman just broken out of prison.

"Will you be back?" she had asked.

"I don't know."

He *didn't* know. He had slept little. Serena's body was there; she was there, begging for him and he had ravished her when the need became too great. Yet he knew he had no business being there.

Not then. With everything hanging over them like an axe about to fall.

Shortly before dawn, Gunn had made up his mind to track down Soo Li. He had a hunch that following her trail would lead him right to Torreon. But where did Carrie Roberts fit in? She had gotten him into this mess

194

in the first place. Almost as if she had planned it that way. Looking back on their meeting, it all looked so damned slick. A bunch of rowdies roughing up a Mexican. Beautiful woman comes waltzing in. Brave hero saves the lady, gets invited to her house, takes her to bed. Not an unfamiliar pattern to Gunn, but this time it was all too pat. There was a kink in the rope somewhere.

Gunn saw the smoke rising straight up in the breezeless air.

The sun was now only a pale globe behind the clouds, but the smoke was plain enough.

Palomas loomed ahead.

"Come on, horse, get your legs." Gunn jabbed the animal in the flanks with the rounded spurs. The horse became all muscle and flying feet.

Gunn knew where the smoke was coming from and his heart sank like a stone.

The Golden Bull!

The tall man guided the horse to the rear of the restaurant. The town appeared to be asleep. There were no people he could see. No shouts of alarm.

He reined up, saw that the smoke was just curling out of the back windows. No flames.

But, there was a hell of a lot of smoke!

"Fire!" Gunn yelled. "Fire!"

That's when the back door burst open.

Gunn stared at the man carrying the torch in one hand. Then, he looked at the man's other hand.

Gunn ducked, as the man fired.

A .44 ball whistled over his head. Stiffened the hackles on his neck. Gunn's hand shot to the butt of his Colt. He drew in a single smooth motion, leaned over his horse's withers.

He recognized the arsonist.

The same Irishman he'd seen in El Paso. Paddy Ryan!

Paddy tossed the torch straight at Gunn's horse, fired two more quick shots.

The horse reared up just as Gunn took aim. His shot went wild as he tumbled backwards, his left hand clawing for purchase on the saddle horn. The torch struck the horse in the chest and he bucked, throwing Gunn forward, off-balance.

The ground came up fast.

Gunn hit the dirt headlong, managed to hold on to his pistol.

"You sonofabitch!" Paddy exclaimed, firing blindly at Gunn's sprawled form.

Gunn's head rattled from the impact. His neck felt as if it had been cracked with a whip.

People, jarred awake, began shouting. He heard the crackle of flames now, felt the heat as the building caught fire in earnest. Scrambling to get away from the bullets, Gunn rolled, brought his own .45 up with both hands.

Paddy ran toward a steeldust gray horse, ground-tied a hundred yards down the alley.

Gunn hammered back, held a low bead on the fleeing Irishman.

The Colt boomed in his hand. The explosion deafened him momentarily.

Paddy stumbled, turned.

Gunn saw the Irishman's pistol blossom fire and the bullet kicked dust into his eyes. The dirt stung, blinded him.

When he regained his vision, Paddy was mounted, jerking a rifle free of its scabbard. Gunn hammered back again, fired off a shot without aiming too tight. He hoped the shot would slow Ryan down, give him a chance to take cover before that rifle opened up on him.

Paddy never flinched.

Instead, he took aim. Over Gunn's head.

Puzzled, the sprawled man looked over his shoulder.

The rifle cracked.

The Mexican horse staggered, blood gushing from its chest.

"You dirty bastard," Gunn muttered.

He swung around, thumbed back the hammer of the Colt and drew a bead on Paddy. He was hoping for a chest shot. At first he had thought only to wound the man so that he could get some information on him. But now that the bastard had shot a horse, he would show no mercy.

Just as Gunn fired again, Paddy wheeled his steeldust gray and put the spurs to his flanks.

Gunn braced himself as the pistol slammed his hand, kicked up from the force of the explosion.

The shot went wide. Way wide.

Paddy galloped off, disappeared.

Gunn rose to his feet as men came racing around the corner of the building. Some carried blankets, another a bucket. They shouted at him, but he ignored them. Paddy was getting away Scot-free and he had no horse.

The Mexican horse was thrashing, in pain.

"Gunn!"

Jed Randall came running up, out of breath.

"What the hell's going on?"

"In a minute," said Gunn. He walked over to the horse, cocked the Colt and fired a bullet into its brain. The horse kicked twice, spasmed, then lay still.

"Jesus, Gunn," said Randall, "all hell's broke loose." He looked at the burning building. Flame shadows

197

flickered over his face. Gunn shoved out the hulls of his spent bullets, flicked fresh ones in the empty chambers.

"Paddy Ryan set the restaurant afire. Got clean away. But I think I wounded the bastard."

"Ryan? Works for Torreon?"

"The same. I'm going after him, soon as I can get another mount. Help me get this gear off of that dead horse."

The two men stripped saddle, blanket, bridle from the Mexican horse. Gunn swung the saddle over his shoulder, grabbed the blanket and bridle from Jed. Men were trying to get a bucket brigade organized to put out the fire, but it was too late. The flames were raging out of control. The wood boards crackled and popped as the fire ate away at everything flammable. Smoke now hovered on the rooftop, seeped through the shingles.

"Anybody inside?" someone asked Gunn.

"I don't know," he replied. He hoped not.

"Want me to come with you?" Randall asked him.

Gunn shook his head.

"Want you to tell Serena Paxton what happened here this morning. Tell her I'm going to track Ryan and try to find Soo Li, see what she knows about all this."

"Soo Li? You can't be serious. Why, that little old gal wouldn't. . . ."

"No, but she's mixed up in this some way. You tell Serena what I said. Tell her she can probably find me at Carrie Roberts' in the next day or so."

"Damn, Gunn," Randall puffed as he followed alongside Gunn toward the livery, "I wish you'd stop talking in circles. Carrie Roberts isn't in this."

"No? Maybe not. But Soo Li was supposed to be there yesterday and neither woman was home when Serena

198

stopped by."

Randall threw up his hands, stopped in his tracks.

Gunn went on, leaving his friend behind. He hadn't worked it all out himself, but now he had Paddy on the run, probably packing a bullet in his leg. A wounded man would run to a safe place. Gunn was mighty curious about where the Irishman would hole up. He wouldn't follow him too close. Let him think he was safe. That was the way to do it. Paddy might be smarter than he figured, but was hurting now. A .45 slug had a way of making a man want to crawl into a blanket and never come out—if it was lodged anyplace under a man's hide.

****

Gunn followed the blood spoor out of Palomas.

From the looks of it, he figured he must have nicked an artery in Paddy Ryan's leg.

There were splotches of blood for a good mile after leaving the town.

Then, the blood trail thinned out. He found the place where Paddy had stopped, evidently to cut himself a tourniquet to stop the bleeding. It didn't make any difference. His horse had left droppings that were still steaming.

He kept looking at the sky, hoping it would not rain. The clouds were darker than before and the land had a gray cast to it. A stillness that almost always preceded a storm. The air felt heavy, wet. The horse under him was a good mount, bought for a hundred dollars in a hurry. A mottled strawberry roan, the animal had good legs and wind. From the looks of his teeth, he was about six years old. The stableman said the horse's name was Chico and

Gunn thought that was a good enough name and the price was cheap enough under the circumstances.

He looked back once, saw the pall of smoke hanging in the sky. When he had left, men were trying to water down the nearby buildings to keep them from going up. He hoped they had made it. A fire in Palomas would put a finish to the town. Damn Ryan anyway. Damn Torreon for putting the Irisher up to it.

The tracks headed for El Paso, then veered off, heading south, toward the border.

Some of the country looked familiar.

Later, he realized why, when he looked down from a chunk of high ground and saw Carrie Roberts' spread. It looked different from that height, but he recognized it. He didn't have time to dawdle, but he looked for signs of life. Nothing. No horses, no one about. Riding on, he saw Ryan's tracks lead onto a well-used trail. The man had made no attempt to hide his tracks. In a few minutes he realized why.

Paddy had stopped again. There was a pool of blood in the dirt.

Gunn dismounted, traced a finger through the mixture of soil and blood. The blood was still slightly warm.

Five minutes, he figured.

Paddy was no more than five minutes away. Evidently his tourniquet had loosened and the man had stopped to tie it tighter. Checking, he saw that he had missed several gouts of blood. Which could mean that some of it dripped down the horse's leg before it accumulated enough to drip off the horse and onto the ground.

Gunn mounted up, and put the spurs to Chico.

The roan cantered down the dusty narrow trail. Easy going now. Gunn let the horse have its head until the trail

200

took a sharp bend. He hauled in on the reins, not wanting to ride into an ambush. He stopped, listened. It was graveyard quiet.

On the other side of the bend, Gunn sucked in a quick breath.

Below him, in a hidden valley, stood several adobes, scattered over a large area. Smoke rose through chimneys in a couple of them. He saw an armed man walk down the main street, disappear into one of the shacks. A dog barked. Beyond, he saw the outline of El Paso, far in the distance.

"Handy," he muttered to himself.

He was certain that Paddy Ryan had holed up in the small settlement. He counted six adobes, a few shacks made of straw and makeshift lumber. It looked to be a hideout. An outlaw town where a man's life wasn't worth much if he happened to be an outsider.

It would not do to ride in, ask questions.

Gunn considered the problem.

He wanted Paddy. Wanted him bad. But he also wanted Torreon and the strangler. Paddy might talk if he put pressure on him. He was wounded, would need medical attention. The longer he holed up, the better his chances to escape without punishment.

He backed Chico off, began scouting a place to leave the horse while he slipped into the town on foot.

A half mile away, he found an arroyo that would serve his purpose. There was grass and water in a hollowed out rock. He slipped the Winchester from its scabbard, filled his pockets with ammunition. If there was going to be a shoot-out, he wanted to give a good accounting of himself.

Tooth throbbing, Gunn set out for the adobe village on

201

foot. He took a different path, circling above the settlement. He wanted to come in from the other side, the blind side where his chances of discovery would be lessened. He kept low, made good time.

Topping a small knoll, he saw a roof less than 300 yards from his position. He crawled on his belly through the bushes to give himself a better view. The settlement was quiet. The clouds continued to blacken and a light breeze began to rattle the mesquite, hum through the cactus. He tasted the wetness of the air. Soon, he knew, there would be a downpour. The rain might work to his advantage at that. At least it would keep everyone inside while he prowled behind the shacks, listening for a clue to Ryan's whereabouts.

Gunn moved off to his right, crawling backwards. He had spotted a game trail that would bring him up behind one adobe that had a single curtained window. A starting place.

The rain hit just before Gunn stalked up to the adobe.

It came down hard, raking the land with driving lances. The air turned colder and the wind began to shriek over the roofs. He heard muffled voices, gruff masculine voices, as men got their animals under cover, fled inside shacks to escape the deluge. He wondered now if Chico would be safe in the arroyo. This was a land of devastating flash floods, quick torrents that could wash a horse away in a rushing torrent as if it was a toy.

He crept to another shack, heard groaning inside.

The rain now slanted hard against the earthen walls of the adobe, drowning out the sounds from within.

Gunn held the rifle straight down to keep water out of the barrel. Now, he cocked it halfway, slipped around the side of the shack.

The rain stung his face, blinded him as he stepped into the open.

Quickly, he stepped to the door. It was ajar.

He thumbed the Winchester to full cock.

Bending low, swinging the barrel of the rifle up, he kicked the door wide open, bulled his way inside.

His shape threw a shadow over the man lying in the corner.

Paddy Ryan's trouser leg was ripped off to his thigh, his bare leg glistening in the lantern light.

He lay there, half-sitting, a bottle of *mezcal* in one hand. His pistol lay out of its holster, within reach.

Paddy looked up at Gunn, his eyes bleary with pain. He licked dry lips.

Gore ran down his leg, and Gunn saw a splinter of bone sticking through the skin.

Paddy's hand started spidering toward the pistol.

"Don't try it," Gunn said quietly.

"Bejesus," said Paddy, "you goin' to shoot me?"

"Not if you talk and say the right things."

"I'm dyin', man. I need a doc."

Gunn looked at the leg again. He would lose that, likely. It was already a blue-green color. He might live if. . . .

"Some answers, first, Ryan."

"You know me name. Fine, fine." He took a swig of *mezcal*, choked on it. Gunn slipped close to him, knelt down, the rifle barrel aimed at Paddy's chest.

"Who is she, Paddy? Tell me quick."

"Ah, you know, then? It's a name you want?"

"Yes, her name. The strangler."

"Jesus. No, that's not her name. You know her. It's. . . ."

203

Paddy's eyes widened.

The explosion boomed inside the adobe.

Paddy's head blew apart as the lead ball parted his skull just above his nose. Blood flew everywhere, spattering Gunn.

Gunn swung the rifle, as Paddy slumped over, dead.

He saw a small form, a figure dressed in black.

Then, only an open doorway with silver streaks of rain dripping off the roof.

As he scrambled to his feet, he heard pounding hoofbeats above the roar of the rain.

Outside, he saw a horse gallop away, down the middle of what passed for a street.

He raised the rifle, but the rain blew needles into his eyes. He wiped them dry, and when he opened them, the rider was gone.

A man stepped out of an adobe, pistol in hand.

Gunn swung on him, even as he saw orange flame blossom from the pistol.

CHAPTER TWENTY

Gunn squeezed the trigger of the Winchester as he went into a crouch.

The rifle bucked in his hand.

A bullet smacked into the adobe, scant inches from his head.

Chunks of adobe bit into his neck, but he saw the Mexican go down, grabbing his gut with both hands. A wide crimson stain spread over the man's white shirt and trousers.

Gunn cranked another round into the chamber, stepped back into the doorway, his eyes darting in every direction.

The rain's din was the only sound.

Gunn waited, but no one came for him. He watched every window, every doorway, for movement.

The rain pattered on until he heard its undertones, its separate sounds as it rattled on the roof, dripped from the eaves.

Paddy was dead. Killed before he could tell Gunn the name of the strangler. At least he hadn't denied that the assassin was a woman. In fact, his eyes had widened when Gunn had told him that much.

A woman. . . .

Strong, self-reliant, able to kill a grown man by twisting a rope around the neck. Shutting off the wind. Watching his eyes bulge, his neck veins rise blue out of the flesh, thicken and throb. Jesus! What kind of a woman could do such a thing and not get sick. Sick unto death. Only a woman who hated much, who did not value human life. A woman who hated men.

Soo Li? Serena? Winifred? Carrie? Patzy Summers?

Gunn thought of them now as he watched for another gunman. He was losing time, but he had to think it all out. He had made love to all but Winifred. None had seemed like man-haters. All right. But what of greed? Which one had the most to gain? And why was Luna Creek property so valuable?

The more questions he asked himself, the more came to him.

He could wait no longer. Whoever had killed Paddy had known he would be there. Had tracked him or figured he would track Paddy.

And, the person was getting away. The strangler? Probably. Likely.

Gunn stepped back outside. He was soaking wet, so he no longer minded the rain. The chill was something, though. It burned through to his bones, made them ache. His tooth was like a stone chisel in his gum. Pounding, throbbing. He vowed that he would pull it as soon as he got his hands on a pair of pliers. And a good bottle of whiskey.

No one showed. Gunn made his way to the next adobe, rifle at the ready, its barrel canted down to keep water from the barrel. Even a little accumulation could be trouble. Any barrel obstruction might cause the breech to blow, or balloon out the barrel. Either way, he'd be without a rifle, and maybe part of his face as well.

Gunn went through the thin door, swept the room with the rifle barrel.

Empty.

He went into each adobe, checking.

In one of them, he found a woman, old and fat, her teeth rotted away. She trembled in fear.

"Where is Torreon?" he asked, in Spanish.

"No sabe."

Gunn left her there. She had started to cry and he knew he wouldn't get anything out of her.

He found two women and a girl in another shack.

They wouldn't talk either.

"What is this place called?" he asked.

"Lunita," said the young girl.

"Do you know Torreon?"

She shook her head.

He knew she was lying, but it was useless to waste time with any of them. They were frightened and probably didn't know much.

In the last shack he checked, Gunn's jaw dropped. Then, his stomach twisted into knots.

It was full of ammunition crates. Freshly broken open. Some shells had been dropped, scattered. Rifle and pistol ammo. Enough to start a war. The knot in his stomach hardened, turned to a cold lead ball.

Outside, he saw the sickening maze of tracks. The rain had almost wiped them out, but he saw them. And, farther on, horse tracks. A labyrinth of small craters full of water. Vees rising up like tiny islands, and circles where the hooves had struck.

He started running, then, his boots slipping in mud,

the puddles splattering against his pantlegs. Toward the arroyo where Chico was ground tied. If his hunch was right, there was no time to waste.

****

Torreon halted the column.

Men and horses ground to a stop. Rubio Amargo flexed his gloved hands, fingers.

"We will divide in two here," Don Diego said. One group to the north. One to the south. We will cross Luna Creek here. "I will go with the south. Rubio with the north. When I give the signal, ride down into Palomas. Kill them all. Leave no one alive!"

A cheer rose up, a gurgling cry washed away by the rain.

"Good!" shouted Torreon. "You hear me!"

"We hear you!" answered a chorus of voices.

"*Vamanos!*"

Fifteen men followed Amargo across Luna Creek and made a beeline for the low ridge that would bring them behind Palomas. Torreon and a dozen men turned an abrupt left and galloped through mud to a point south of the town.

Soon, the two lines of men disappeared from sight of each other.

Torreon was stopped, moments later, by a grumbling in ranks. Then, he heard the sound. What the men were talking about.

A lone rider crested the ridge, came bearing down on the creek.

"Hold up, don't shoot!" shouted Torreon, above the storm.

The horse and rider did not cross the creek.

Instead, the rider pulled up, stood in the stirrups.

"Gunn! He is in Lunita!" shouted the rider.

"Did you kill him?" shouted back Torreon.

"No! He is coming!"

"How soon?"

"An hour. Less."

"Go back to the rancho. Wait for me there."

"I—I'm afraid!"

"We will do it. *Venceremos!*"

The men cheered.

"Papa! He knows! He knows who I am!"

"How?"

"I don't know. He just knows!"

"Then ride with us!"

"No. I will face him. I will kill him!"

"*Viva!*" shouted Torreon.

"*Viva. Caridad!*" echoed his men through the patter-slosh of rain.

Torreon shook his fist and rode on. The woman on the other side of the bank sat in her saddle a long time watching the men ride on. Her tears mingled with the rain on her face.

"Papa," she breathed. "Hurry back."

Then, ruthlessly, she rammed Mexican-roweled spurs into her horse's flanks and rode east through the blistering slant of rain, the wind bashing against her poncho, threatening to unseat her from the saddle.

* * * * * * *

Gunn rode Chico hard.

Small floods blocked his path now and then, but he

knew which way to go. The tracks of thirty-odd horses was plain to follow, even in the storm. Where the horses had passed, a wide, shallow river ran like a miniature torrent.

He crossed the swollen creek, saw the mass of tracks split up. There was no longer any question of what he had to do.

"I hope you got it in you, Chico," he said.

The roan responded to his spurs. Gunn took him to the high ground, drier than the route Torreon had taken.

Palomas had less than an hour to live if he didn't reach it in time.

****

Jed Randall's face was smeared with lampblack. His hat brim dripped water in front of his face.

The fire at The Golden Bull smouldered in the rain. Portions of the walls still stood, but the inside of the building was gutted.

He had left the Paxton ranch less than an hour ago, seen Serena take the south fork road to Carrie Roberts' place. He assumed that Gunn would meet her there. That's why he was surprised to see Gunn come racing down the street, hell bent for leather.

"Whoa!" Jed hollered. "Fire's out."

"Like hell it is! Torreon's coming with about thirty or forty men. Better get this town tucked in and ready!"

"No shit?"

Gunn looked at Jed with an icy stare as he slid the Winchester from its scabbard and climbed down out of the saddle.

"Get to it, Jed," said Gunn, leading Chico toward the

210

stable. "Get 'em all in on this. Jimbo's in five minutes. I'll tell 'em how we're going to do it."

"You just take right over, don't you, man?"

"You got a question, Jed?"

"Reckon not."

Gunn saw as many men as he could, while Jed ran up and down, rousting out tired men who had worked for hours trying to keep the town from burning down. They stood inside Jimbo's Emporium with soot-streaked faces, as the rain rattled on the roof and clattered against the windows.

"Less than a half hour," Gunn said, "until Torreon rides in here to wipe out the town. Two groups, one from the north, one from the south. You keep 'em out in the open, fight'll peter out quicker. I need twenty men to ride with me. We'll clamp the group from the north in a pincers, cut 'em to pieces before they can take cover. Any volunteers?"

There were perhaps forty or fifty men and women there. Jimbo "appointed" twenty to ride with Gunn. He split these into two groups, laid out their plan of action once the signal was given.

"Rest of you, split up and take up positions in the back of the buildings. Stay low, use loaders if you can. Keep the rifles hot on the south and I'll bring my men in as soon as we've killed or run off the bunch coming in from the north."

Men grumbled and muttered, but Gunn knew they would do what he asked. It was their town and it was all the future most of them had.

Gunn had men waiting on both ends of town.

He did not have long to wait.

Amargo's band swooped down on Palomas with wild

211

hoarse cries. Shooting from two hundred yards, they figured surprise was on their side.

Gunn let them come. No shots were fired until the Mexicans were right on top of the outlying buildings. Then, men inside opened up, cutting down two or three raiders in the first volley. Amargo's men didn't panic. They were well-trained. Men concentrated their fire power on those places where the shots had thinned their ranks.

Gunfire erupted on the south side of town and Gunn knew he'd have to move fast.

He rode out, fired a rifle shot in the air. Nine men charged with him as they picked off Torreon's men one by one. Ahead, ten other men came riding full tilt straight toward him.

Amargo yelled, but his words were lost above the noise and smoke of battle.

A Mexican screamed.

Gunn took one out with a shot from the hip at close range. He could almost hear the bone splinter from the bullet's impact. He shot another man who was trying to escape up the hill.

The fire fighting on the south side grew more fierce. Gunn knew he could wait no longer.

He raised his rifle, signalled to the others.

Out of the corner of his eye, he saw a riderless horse race up the hill.

Something clicked in his mind.

"Other side!" he yelled above the din. "Torreon's there!"

The two groups reformed and rode toward the south. With luck, Gunn thought, they ought to catch the other attackers out in the open on unprotected flanks.

The riderless horse caught his eye again.

It had a rider. Rubio Amargo sat up in the saddle, shook his fist at Gunn.

Gunn let him go. He couldn't lose the town over one man.

The flank attacks caught Torreon by surprise. Gunn and his men began systematically cutting down the raiders. Those in the town ran out to share in the glory and Torreon knew he was finished. He had failed to take over Palomas.

Gunn saw him ride off, three other men protecting his rear, and knew that he still had to face him down. Men were cheap in that part of the country, over the border. Torreon would bring a hundred next time. And if that didn't work, he'd bring a thousand.

"Jed," Gunn called. "Want to take a little ride?"

Jed looked up, a grin smeared over his blackened face.

"Hell yes. Haven't had this much fun since the hogs ate my baby brother."

"Torreon got away. Not much fun, but a little action, maybe."

"You know where he's gone?"

"I have a strong hunch."

Jed's grin faded away.

"Yeah," he said. "I know about your damned hunches. Somebody else is gonna die this day. I'll guarandoubletee it!"

Gunn's look told him there was more hell coming.

CHAPTER TWENTY-ONE

Gunn and Jed, on fresh horses, looked down at the Roberts house which was dripping with falling rain.

"Why would Torreon go there?"

"I don't know, Jed. But, look at that baby river runnin' down toward the house. That's a trail and that trail leads right to a place called Lunita, which is Torreon's hidey hole. You hear any bells ringing?"

"Hell, yes. Looks to me like this was set up thataway."

"Probably was. Carrie Roberts owns land in Luna Creek Valley, but I checked it at Paxton's. It's a checkerboard holding and not much of it prime. A foothold, though, and some sections might be called strategic."

"Winifred showed you the grant deeds?"

"Serena did."

Jed looked at Gunn with admiration.

"Damned if that isn't where you spent last night. Uh, Gunn?"

"Let's get moving. You take the back, I'll take the front. You hear me shooting, you go busting right in."

"They'll be waiting for us," Jed mused.

"They won't do anything until they realize there are

214

only two of us. I think Torreon and Amargo are probably hiding inside. If my hunch is right, the woman will try to bluff us out."

"Which woman?"

Gunn smiled.

****

There were three Mexicans guarding the front of the house.

The rain kept them under cover.

They didn't see Gunn until he was right on top of them.

His Colt was in his hand, cocked. He merely tipped up the barrel, squeezed the trigger and one Mexican fell headfirst over the low adobe wall. Gunn swung the barrel slightly as he hammered back, shot the second man in the gut. The third saw Gunn's shadowy figure in the rain thick gloom and wanted no part of him. Blood mixed with water in the garden where the second Mexican lay, eyes open, mouth filling up with falling rain.

The third man threw his pistol down, ran right past Gunn.

Gunn swung on him, shot him in the back.

"If that's the way you want to die, bastard, so be it," he muttered.

The door opened.

Carrie Roberts stood there, petite, lovely.

"What's the shooting all about?"

"You had some vermin in your garden."

Gunn ejected the empty hulls, slid fresh bullets in his gun. He shoved the pistol back in the holster, went inside.

Jed was already there, dripping on Carrie's rug.

"Didn't see a soul," he said. "Just walked right on in here."

Gunn looked at Soo Li, sitting primly on a chair, dressed in a silk kimona, her dark hair braided in a single pigtail.

"Soo Li."

Serena looked at Gunn from another chair. She held a tea cup in her lap.

"Serena. Glad you could make it."

"Gunn, may I get you and Jed some brandy?" Carrie seemed oblivious to the fact that both men looked like drowned rats. "Sit down by the fire, dry out." The fire crackled in the hearth, but Gunn didn't look at it. He could cut the tension in the room with a knife.

"No brandy," he told Carrie. "We won't be long. Jed, come here. I got something to say to you private."

Jed sloshed over. Gunn whispered something in his ear. Jed nodded, then left the room.

"What was it, Carrie?" Gunn asked, standing now with his back to the fire. "Just land? Or something else? Oil? Gold? Silver?"

"I have no idea what you're talking about, Gunn."

"Yes you do. I thought it might be Soo Li, but it's you. Torreon set this up a long time ago. I just don't see how you could kill your own husband. Strangle him to death."

"Gunn!" admonished Serena.

Soo Li sat silent, like a cat, watching Gunn's face.

"Really, this is perfectly ridiculous," said Carrie. "You have a nerve, insulting me in my own home."

Gunn reached a hand inside his shirt. He pulled out the length of rope he had found in Soo Li's restaurant.

216

"Recognize this, Carrie? You meant to use it on me. I reckon Jed will find some more rope just like it in your bedroom. Maybe the clothes you wore today. Probably still wet."

Carrie's face paled.

Gunn pulled the torn piece of cloth from his pocket.

"If this matches up. . . ." he said.

Jed stomped into the room carrying the things Gunn had sent him to look for. Wet black silk garments, a rope, a diary.

Gunn put the piece of cloth up to the hole in the silk jacket. It matched perfectly.

"Are these your clothes, Soo Li?" Gunn switched his attention suddenly to the Chinese woman.

"Yes, but. . . ."

"I know. You and Carrie are about the same size. You left these here and she's been wearing them. At night. She was able to get close to those men because they never thought a woman meant them harm. Carrie killed your father, Serena. And the others."

Gunn took the diary from Jed's hand.

"You look in it like I told you?"

Jed nodded.

"It was gold and silver. You were right, Gunn."

"Where?"

"South of Luna Creek. Well within the survey boundaries."

Carrie's face blanched.

"Papa!" she screamed.

Don Diego Torreon burst into the room, pistol blazing.

Soo Li rose from her chair, caught a bullet in the breast.

Gunn's hand streaked to his Colt. As Jed turned to

draw, Gunn fired at Torreon. Jed's pistol was halfway out as Torreon hit the floor, skidding backwards from the force of the bullet. He clutched his heart, but his eyes were already clouding over. His mouth worked like a gasping fish's.

"Look out, Jed!" Gunn warned.

El Guante appeared in the hall doorway, a pistol in his hand.

Jed cleared leather, cocked his pistol, fired.

A small hole appeared in Rubio Amargo's forehead. A look of surprise flooded his face for a moment. He stood fast, teetered, then toppled forward.

Carrie ran toward the door.

Serena ran after her, threw herself headlong at Carrie's rump. Falling short, she tackled the woman. Carrie and Serena fell to the floor. Serena's face was contorted in rage. Savagely, she crawled up Carrie's back, grabbed her hair and pulled.

Carrie screamed in pain.

Serena jerked Carrie's head, flipped her over.

Then, she struck.

Her hands shot to Carrie's throat, closed tightly on her windpipe.

Carrie's face turned blue.

"You murdered my father!" screamed the hysterical Serena.

Gunn pulled her off.

"Not that way," he said gently. "She'll swing from a rope anyway. She'll die the same way your father did. But legal."

Carrie began sobbing as her breath returned. She huddled up in a ball as Serena looked down at her without pity.

"What was Torreon to you, Carrie?" Gunn asked.

"My—my father."

"Your father?"

"Yes. My name was Caridad Torreon."

"Jesus," said Jed.

Soo Li moaned. Gunn went to her. She was dying. Squatting beside her, he picked her up, held her in his arms.

Serena came and stood over them as Jed held his pistol aimed at Carrie.

"I—I love you, Gunn," whispered Soo Li.

Tears swam in Gunn's eyes.

"I love you too, Soo Li."

"You love Soo Li."

He nodded, fighting back the tears.

"That is much happiness for me."

Serena winced as Soo Li choked. The Chinese woman gave a sigh, and went slack in Gunn's arms. He lay her down gently, stood up.

Serena looked at him oddly.

"Did you love her?" she asked.

"She was a good woman."

"That's no answer, Gunn."

"It's all the answer I know right now." He turned away from her. "I'll have that brandy Carrie offered." He headed for the sidebar, found a bottle, poured four fingers into a glass. "You have a pair of pliers, Carrie?"

Carrie sat up, dazed.

"Pliers?"

"Yeah. I've got a tooth that won't wait."

"In—in the tack room, I think."

"Jed, bring 'em," said Gunn. He helped Carrie to her feet as Jed holstered his pistol, stalked from the room. A few minutes later, he was back, a pair of pliers in his hand. Most of Gunn's glass was empty. He poured another four fingers, drank it, holding on to the sidebar.

Jed handed him the pliers.

"You're not going to pull your own tooth?" he asked.

"Gunn, that's terrible," said Serena, stunned.

Gunn said nothing. He put the pliers to the offending tooth. Pain shot through him like a fire. He closed his eyes, gave the pliers a twist. He heard a cracking sound in his head. The pain blotted out his senses, bloomed in his mind like a torch. His knees buckled.

He twisted some more, felt the tooth loosen. He gave a hard yank and cried out in a muffled voice. The tooth came free. He held the bloody stump up for Jed to see.

Serena swooned.

"Grab her," Gunn said, thick-tongued.

Jed caught her before she hit the floor. Just barely.

Gunn grinned. The pain was gone. A dull ache, where the tooth had been, replaced it.

"You're quite a man, aren't you, Gunn?" mocked Carrie. "You know that Serena's in love with you, don't you?"

"No."

"You could be a rich man if you marry her."

"I'll be riding on," he said. "After I watch you hang."

"Will you bury my father decent?"

"As decent as he deserves."

"I—I think I loved you, too," she whispered.

"Just one thing, Carrie. Who tried to strangle me in my hotel room? It wasn't you."

"No. It was. . . ."

The shot blotted out the name on Carrie's lips. She stumbled forward, a bullet in her back. The window

220

shattered and glass spewed onto the floor.

Gunn drew, cocked and fired. Twice. A man toppled forward, smashing more glass. He lay face down on the floor.

Serena's eyes opened.

She stood up, stared at the man on the floor. A pool of blood fed by a stream coming from the dead man's chest began to form on the edge of a rug. Jed walked toward the man, bent down.

"Don't you know who it is, Jed?" Gunn asked.

Jed looked at him, shook his head.

"You know, don't you, Serena?"

Serena brought a hand to her mouth. She stared at Gunn in horror.

"No!" she gasped.

"Yes, Serena. The inside man. Hank Worley."

Jed flipped the man over.

Worley's eyes stared up at them vacantly.

"He was the man who tried to put me under that night at the hotel," said Gunn. "He was in cahoots with Torreon. There had to be an inside man. Carrie was too far out of it to do much, except kill. Worley was greedy."

"But . . . how . . . ?" asked Jed.

"He was the only man who didn't lose any cattle. Trying to cover himself. He wasn't much of a man. He thought he'd steal a page from Carrie's book, get me out of the way. It didn't work. He was a coward, to boot."

Gunn tossed his tooth through the window.

Serena staggered to a chair, collapsed.

Gunn looked at her with tenderness.

It wouldn't work out, he thought. *There's too much blood between us. But she was the best.*

Someday, maybe. But not now.

"Come on, Jed," he said. "Let's clean this mess up. I'm half drunk and feeling no pain."

"I need some of that brandy myself," Jed told him.

"Help yourself. It's on the house!"

Serena stared at the two men, her face white as flour.

"In some ways, Gunn," she said, "you're just as cruel as these people were. Just as heartless. Don't you feel anything?"

Gunn sucked in a breath, began to reload his Colt.

"What do you think, Serena?" he asked.

Serena looked at him, then bowed her head. Her shoulders began to shake as the tears came.

"Better pour some brandy for Serena too," Gunn said quietly.